It's a funny thing how it takes your emotions much longer than your intellect to realize it when some big change happens in your life. My feeling this new numb way about my parents was the biggest change that had ever happened to me and I couldn't get used to it. All that week I'd wake up in the morning and know that something was wrong and my mind had to tell my heart that it was because my mother had talked to Jacques on the phone, because my parents were Rose and Rafferty Dickinson instead of just Mother and Father. Then my heart would try to adjust itself to unhappiness, but still it didn't realize why it was unhappy and it instinctively turned to Mother for comfort, and then my mind would say, "No, you mustn't do that anymore." And gradually my heart began to know what my mind had been telling it every day: that everything was changed, that nothing could ever be the same again.

MADELEINE L'ENGLE is the author of numerous books, including the Newbery Award–winning *A Wrinkle in Time*, *A Wind in the Door*, and *A Swiftly Tilting Planet*. Her most recent novel, *A Ring of Endless Light*, was named a Newbery Honor Book. It is the third volume of the Austin Family Trilogy, which also includes *Meet the Austins* and *The Moon by Night*. All are available in Dell Laurel-Leaf editions. Madeleine L'Engle lives in New York City with her husband.

Camilla

MADELEINE L'ENGLE

LAUREL-LEAF BOOKS bring together under a single imprint outstanding works of fiction and nonfiction particularly suitable for young adult readers, both in and out of the classroom. Charles F. Reasoner, Professor Emeritus of Children's Literature and Reading, New York University, is consultant to this series.

Published by
Dell Publishing Co., Inc.
1 Dag Hammarskjold Plaza
New York, New York 10017

To Hugh Franklin

This book was originally published in another version under the title of *Camilla Dickinson*.

Laurel-Leaf Library ® TM 766734, Dell Publishing Co., Inc.

ISBN: 0-440-91171-0

RL: 5.3

Reprinted by arrangement with Delacorte Press
Printed in the United States of America
First Laurel-Leaf printing—December 1982
Fourth Laurel-Leaf printing—September 1984

.... **Camilla** ....

I

I knew as soon as I got home on Wednesday that Jacques was there with my mother. I knew it when I walked into the entrance hall of the apartment and the doorman said, "Good afternoon, Miss Camilla," and smiled at me with the eager and curious smile for which I had begun to look each time I came home. I walked across the hall, and prayed that Jacques would go now that I was home, that he would go before my father came. And I was glad that I had come straight home after school instead of going for a walk with Luisa.

I stepped into the elevator and the elevator boy said, as though he had something exotic-tasting in his mouth, "Good afternoon, Miss Camilla. You have company upstairs."

"Oh?" I said.

"Yes."

The elevator boy is small and fat and, though he has white hair and two of his teeth are missing and show black gaps in his mouth, he is always called the elevator boy; never the elevator man. And the way his eyes are always dancing with something malicious in them when he talks makes him seem much more like the brothers of some of the girls at school than like a grown person. His eyes had that nasty happiness in them now, as though he were about to put out a foot and trip me up and then roar with laughter when he saw me fall on my face.

"That Mr. Nissen is upstairs," he said, grinning. "He asked especially if you was in and then he said he'd go upstairs and wait for you."

Yes, I could hear in my mind's ear how Jacques would ask for me, smiling and speaking in that voice of his as soft as a spaniel's ear. Yes, I am the one Jacques always asks for. I am like a game between Jacques and the doorman and the old elevator boy, a ball they throw back and forth between them, always smiling, smiling, as though they all understand the game is quite unimportant. . . .

So the elevator boy looked at me with that giggly look and stopped the elevator at the fourteenth floor. It is really the thirteenth floor, but I have noticed that in most apartment houses they just skip thirteen and call it fourteen. This is silly. You can change the number but you can't change the floor.

I said good-bye to the elevator boy and pulled my

key out of the pocket of my navy blue coat and let myself into the apartment. I could hear their voices from the living room. My mother was laughing, high and excited and happy. Don't ever let my father hear her laugh like that, I begged, but I don't know to whom I was begging, my mother, or Jacques, or God.

I went down the hall to my room and hung up my coat and my red beret and put my schoolbooks down on the desk. Then I did not sit down and start my homework as I usually do when I get in, but went back toward the living room so that Jacques would be sure to know I was home. I walked heavily, clumping my school shoes down on the silver-green carpet so that he would know before I got to the living room. Then I knocked.

"Come in," my mother said. "Oh, it's you, Camilla, darling. How was school? I was saying to Jacques how well you always—your last report card was really— your father and I are most pleased with your progress."

My mother always talks in little rushes, as though she were in such a hurry to say everything that there isn't time ever quite to finish a sentence. Her voice sounds like a brook leaping and tumbling downhill, and broken up and divided by all shapes and sizes of rocks.

I went over to my mother and kissed her and then I shook hands with Jacques. My mother said, "Good heavens, Camilla, your cheek is like ice. Is it raining or— Do you think it will snow tonight, Jacques, it's really time— Of course I don't like snow in the city after— But then it's lovely while it's falling." And then she laughed. I don't know quite what the laugh meant, but I think she just feels free to laugh because she thinks I am so young that I still like a kitten with eyes that aren't ready to open yet. But when you are fifteen you have passed that stage. Fifteen is a strange number of years to be; it is so convenient for my mother and father that I am fifteen because they can always say that I am too young or too old whenever they want to say no about anything. Luisa is sixteen and she says it is the same way with her; you lose all the privileges of being a child and get none of the privileges of being grown-up.

"Good afternoon, Camilla," Jacques said, in that silky way of his. And he looked at my mother. "Yes, Rose, it must have started to rain. Am I right, Camilla?"

"Yes." I pulled my hand out of his. He did not open his fingers but held his hand over mine so that I felt his palm all the way as I slid my fingers out.

"Your lashes are wet," Jacques said, "and there is rain in your hair. I brought you a present, Camilla."

"Oh, yes, Camilla, do look at— Jacques brought you a lovely— Yes, Jacques came to—he dropped by just for you—to bring you a present."

Jacques went to the table that stood under the Carroll portrait of my mother and picked up a package like a small coffin. He gave it to me. "Perhaps you are too old for this, Camilla," he said, "but your mother tells me you are learning to sew this year and—"

"Yes, Camilla is learning to sew so beautifully—it

4

will be lovely for her to practice on—all the little dresses and perhaps even some hats—" my mother cried, her voice high and excited.

"Thank you," I said.

"Aren't you going to open it?" my mother asked me.

I opened the package. It was a doll. A large doll with real hair and long black eyelashes and horrible staring blue eyes that rolled in its head as well as opening and closing. And as I lifted it up its tiny rosy mouth opened and there were two rows of cruel little white teeth. I have never liked dolls. Somehow they have always frightened me a little because they are like cartoons of all that is cold and unloving and uncaring in people.

"You see? She has lashes like yours, Camilla. And she's—she's really not just a doll for a child, you know." He seemed suddenly nervous and he pushed his fingers quickly over his hair, which is thick and wavy and almost as fair as my mother's.

The doll's head lolled against my arm and the round, pink mouth closed in a sneer.

"How about your schoolwork—don't you have homework to do, Camilla? All that Latin—and is it geometry you were asking your father to— I never could understand geometry," my mother said.

"Yes," I said to my mother. "Thank you very much for the doll," I said to Jacques.

I left the room and walked down the hall again. I put the doll down on a chair and it fell over so that it lay with its head on the arm of the chair like a midget who was drunk. Then I remembered I had left the box and the wrappings on the table under my mother's portrait, so I went back to the living room and this time I did not knock. I don't know whether I did this on purpose or not, but when I walked into the room, there were Jacques and my mother kissing, as I had known they would be.

"I forgot the box the doll came in," I said in a loud voice and went over to the table.

Jacques opened his mouth to say something and closed it and then he opened it again and I think that this time he really would have said something, only then we were all frozen into silence by the sound of my father's key in the lock.

We heard my father come in and the soft thud as he tossed his hat on the hall table and his coat on the chair for Carter, the maid, to pick up. Then my mother went over to the sofa and sat down in front of the coffee table and lit a cigarette. Her fingers were as pale and thin as the cigarette and they were trembling. Jacques lit a cigarette, too, and his fingers were not trembling at all.

My father came into the room and he had a tight smile on his face that did not change when he saw Jacques but simply became a little more tight, the way the braces on my teeth feel when I have just been to the dentist.

"Good evening, Rafferty, my love," my mother said,

and squashed out her unsmoked cigarette in an ashtray. The cigarette crumpled and then broke and little bits of tobacco stuck out from the tear. "Camilla says it's raining. Did you get— Hadn't you better change your shoes if— Or has it stopped?"

"It's still raining," my father said, and he leaned across the coffee table and kissed my mother. Then he nodded to Jacques. "Evening."

"What time is—or are you early?" my mother asked him.

"I'm early," my father said. "You're looking very lovely this evening, Rose." Then he smiled that tight smile at me, as though it hurt him to move his mouth. "What have you got there, Camilla?"

"A box," I said.

"And what is the purpose of the box?" My father leaned over the coffee table again, took a cigarette from the silver box, and handed it to my mother. Then he pulled out his lighter and lit it for her. All the while he said nothing and looked at her and she looked back at him with the blue eyes of the doll. And my father seemed to grow until he filled up the whole room, standing by the coffee table in his dark suit, his cigarette lighter still flaring in his outstretched hand.

"It's a box a doll came in," I said.

"A doll?"

Now I knew that Jacques and my mother were glad I had come back into the room when I did. My mother said, "Jacques brought Camilla a doll. Jacques is Camilla's most ardent admirer."

"And where is the doll?" my father asked. "Really, Rose, why on earth would anyone give a doll to Camilla? She's not a child anymore."

This was the first time I had ever heard my father be rude to anyone, and it startled me. I said, "It's in my room. I came back to get the box." I looked at Jacques and then at my mother and then at my father. My father is a very large man. He is tall and broad and his body is as solid as a stone. His hair is as strong and definite as black marble and the streaks of white that touch his temples are like the markings in marble. His shoulders are as broad as the shoulders on the statue of Atlas on Fifth Avenue near Rockefeller Center, the one who is holding up the world and looks as though he is slipping off his pedestal from the weight of it. But my father's foot would not slip.

"Fix you a drink, Nissen?" my father asked.

"Thanks—no," Jacques murmured. "I must be going. I have an appointment downtown."

I did not wait to hear him say good-bye but slipped out of the living room and went back to my room. I turned off the light. At first I could not see anything; for a moment it was like being blind, but then the light came in through my window from the lighted windows of the apartments across the court. I pushed the curtains aside and looked out. When I was much younger I used to think that living on the court was like living partway down the rabbit's hole in *Alice's Adventures in Wonderland*. Sometimes Luisa and I will stand by the window and watch it grow dark and tell each other things about the people who live in the other apartments. Or I will try on clear winter nights to show Luisa the stars. You have to lean far out and look up through the rabbit's hole of buildings to see them, but when it is very cold and clear I can point out Aldebaran and Betelgeuse, Bellatrix and Sirius, the Pleiades and Perseus.

Three sides of the court that form the rabbit's hole are made up of the big apartment house in which I live. The fourth side is a smaller, lower apartment house, and I can see the roof where there is a big tank with a ladder going up to it, but which I have never seen anybody climb. It is across this roof that I can find the most stars. Sometimes on warm days young women will come up onto the roof in bathing suits and spread blankets out and lie in the sun, and in the evening they will come up with young men and watch the moon rise above the broken edges of the city and kiss the way I saw my mother and Jacques kiss. The rooms in this smaller building are different from the ones in our house. They are more cluttered and the people don't bother to pull down their shades or close their venetian blinds as often and there are fewer maids turning on lamps and lighting candles on mahogany tables and bustling around kitchens in the evenings. There is something very comforting about kitchens. It always cheers me up to stand by my bedroom window and watch dinner being cooked and imagine things about happy families with lots of children.

I stood there at my window after I had left my

mother and father and Jacques saying good-bye, and looked through the veil of falling rain into a big kitchen in the smaller house where a whole family, mother and father and four children and a grandmother, too, were sitting around a big blue kitchen table eating scrambled eggs and bacon for supper. Then my door opened and I heard my father's voice.

"Camilla."

I turned around and he was standing, almost filling up the doorway, outlined in warm yellow light from the hall.

"Here I am, Father," I said.

"What are you doing all alone in the dark?"

"Just looking at the rain."

"That's a melancholy business," my father said. "Turn on your light and put on one of your pretty dresses and come out to dinner with me."

"Oh," I said.

"Your mother has a headache," my father said, "so she's going to bed to have tea and toast, and I thought it might be fun for us to go out cavorting together. How about it?"

"Fine." I moved away from the window and turned on the light by my desk, blinking against its sharpness.

"I'll give you half an hour to primp in, and then we'll go." My father gave me a clumsy pat on the shoulder and left me.

I went into the bathroom and took a shower and brushed my teeth. Brushing my teeth is a nuisance because of my braces, though it's easier now that the

10

outside ones are off and I just have them on the inside. While I was brushing my teeth my mother came to the bathroom door in a rose velvet negligee and said, "Camilla darling, when you're dressed, come to my room and—heavens, darling, you've got toothpaste all over your face—and I'll fix your hair for you and you can use some of my makeup." Her face was puckered with anxiety and her eyelashes were just a little damp and stuck-together-looking, as though she had started to cry and then decided against it. Her pale hair was tumbled about her shoulders and it looked softer and more luxuriant than the velvet of her gown. "All right, Camilla darling?"

"All right, Mother," I said, and started to put the top back on the toothpaste. It slipped out of my fingers and rolled like a little round black beetle down the slippery sides of the washbasin and into the drain, where I had to fish and fish for it with my fingers; and all the while my mother stood there in the doorway, looking as though she was about to burst into tears, and watched me.

"You can use my tweezers, darling, to get that nasty top if you— Really, they're lots easier than your fingers." But just then I got the top out and rinsed it off and put it back on the toothpaste.

My mother turned to go, saying as she left, "Do hurry now, darling, and don't keep your father— Rafferty hates to be kept waiting."

I washed my face again to make sure I got all the toothpaste off and went back to my room and dressed.

I put on the sheer smoky stockings my mother had given me for my birthday and which I had never worn before and a dress she had bought me that is neither silver nor green, and that changes color as you move in it. It is a very beautiful dress and the one dress-up thing that I have that I really like and don't feel strange and uncomfortable in. Luisa gets annoyed at me because I care about clothes, but I love pretty things when they seem right for me.

When I went into my mother's room she was lying on her chaise longue with a soft blanket over her knees, but she got up as I came in and stood looking at me. And her face was suddenly very sad.

"Yes," my mother said, "you look very—oh, yes, Camilla darling, you look lovely!" And she pushed the sadness out of her face and wrinkled up her eyes in a smile at me, the way she used to when I was very small.

"Now," she said, "let's—here, put this on, darling," and she handed me a little plastic makeup cape to tie around my shoulders. Then she took her brush off the glass top of her dressing table and started to brush my hair and as she brushed she talked. "Your hair is as black as Rafferty's, Camilla. You look like a little elf, with that solemn peaked face and the black hair and thick bangs. It's too bad your forehead's so high, but then the bangs cover— And those green eyes are very interesting. Did you like the doll Jacques brought you? He came this afternoon just to bring you the doll. Of course you're old for dolls, but then it's such a special— And then he wanted to talk to me because he's terribly unhappy. That wife of his, the things she—oh, I could never tell you, not till you're older, but the life Jacques lived with— And what an unattractive woman, too, so angular and brusque— And now with the divorce and everything—so of course I had to comfort him. Those shoes don't really go with that dress, Camilla. You haven't any that do, though, have you? I must— How would you like to wear my silver shoes tonight? The odd thing is that Jacques thinks I'm so strong. Now that *is* odd, isn't— He doesn't know me the way you and Raff do. But he keeps telling me: Rose, you're the strong one, so I have to pretend to be strong, as though he were a little boy, you know."

I thought of the young men and women on the roof in the summer and on the mild winter nights and I thought of the way my mother had held her arms around Jacques that afternoon. I didn't say anything.

My mother stopped brushing my hair and selected a paintbrush from a bouquet of paintbrushes in a little vase; she twirled it in a small jar of red and painted on my mouth, drawing first the outlines of my lips and then filling them in with quick careful strokes. And she took a little round sheepskin powder puff and brushed it over my lips and then she took the paintbrush and made the shape of my mouth again.

"If Rafferty asks you—" she started, and then she went to her big closet and brought me her silver shoes, "of course I don't know why he would," she said, and took her rabbit's foot, touched it to her rouge, then rubbed it over my cheeks and the very tip of my ears and the tip of my chin. "But if he does," she said, "I know you'll—" She took a string of pearls and hung them around my neck, lifting up my hair in back to fasten the clasp. "But of course I know I can always trust you, my own darling Camilla, because you're a big girl now. You're really grown-up. But if—" and then the telephone rang. She ran to answer it quickly before Carter could get to the extension in the hall. "Hello!" she cried into the mouthpiece. "Oh, hello!" And then her face dropped again into the look of a sad small flower and she said, "It's for you, Camilla. It's Luisa. But don't talk too long because Rafferty— you mustn't keep him waiting."

I went to the telephone and said, "Hello."

"Hello," Luisa said. There was a buzzing on the line and it sounded as though she were calling long-distance instead of from downtown on Ninth Street. Well, Greenwich Village *is* almost a different world from Park Avenue, more exciting, and a little frightening. Luisa's voice came distantly through the buzz. "I guess you're not alone where I can talk to you."

"No," I said.

"Oh, blast. Well, can you come down? Have you had dinner? What about your parents? Mine are both out and Frank and I had a fight and he ate up all my share of the food. Come on down and we can go somewhere and have a hamburger and a milkshake."

"I can't," I said. "I have to— I'm going out to have dinner with my father."

"Oh, blast," Luisa said again. "Well, are you all right? You sound funny."

"I'm okay."

"Well, listen, are you going to get to school early tomorrow?"

"Yes," I said. "I'll have to. I don't think I'll be able to get anywhere near all my homework done tonight."

"Okay," Luisa said. "I'll get there early too."

"Okay," I said. "Good night."

I hung up and turned around and my father was standing waiting by my mother's dressing table and my mother was sitting on the dressing-table stool and looking at him.

"Don't keep Camilla out too long, Raff," she said. "She's still just a baby."

"A very elegant baby, then." My father smiled at me. He looked down at my mother again. "Headache any better?"

She nodded, but carefully, as though it would hurt her head to move it with a jerk. "A tiny bit. But come home to me soon, Rafferty, don't—" She took a bottle of perfume and touched her fingertip to its crystal lip and dabbed a drop behind each of my ears and at my wrists. "Come home to me soon, Raff," she repeated, pleading like a child.

My father kissed her on top of her head, brushing his lips briefly against the softness of her hair. Then he

15

said, "Get on your coat and hat, Camilla. I'll meet you in the hall."

I put on my Sunday coat, which is dark, dark green with a little silver squirrel collar and has a little squirrel muff; and I put on my hat, which is the same green as the coat and has two little squirrel pompons on it, and pulled my white gloves out of the pocket where I had stuffed them the last time I wore the coat. Fortunately they were clean, so I put them on and hurried out to the hall to meet my father. He took my hand and drew it through his arm; his arm felt strong and protecting, as though it ought to have the power to keep things from going wrong. When we got into the elevator, because I was with my father the elevator boy didn't leer at me but just said, "Good evening, Miss Camilla. Good evening, Mr. Dickinson."

Out on the street it was still raining. The rain fell down between the buildings and made a haze about the streetlights and splattered on the sidewalks, and in the streets it lay in rainbow puddles of oil. The sky sagged down between the buildings and I stood there wondering why it is that when it rains at night in New York the sky is a much lighter color than it is on a clear night, and there is always a sickish pink tinge to it.

The doorman had on a slicker and carried an umbrella; when my father and I came out he put his whistle to his lips and blew for a taxi. Taxis came by but they were full; the people in them kept glancing at us standing there on the wet pavement just in the shelter of the building and seemed to be congratulating themselves that they were warmly seated in a taxi while we were standing there in the dark and cold. The canopy that was usually out in front of our apartment building was down to be mended or painted or whatever it is they do to those canopies when they take them down, and the rain poured through the wet, gleaming frame. The doorman kept blowing his whistle and taxis kept rushing by.

"You aren't dressed for walking in the rain, are you, Camilla?" my father asked me.

"Oh, I don't mind. I love to walk in the rain. Luisa and I walk miles in the rain," I said.

My father looked at my little fur muff and collar and the fur pompons on my hat and said, "But not in those clothes. Rose—your mother would be very angry if I let you ruin your brand-new winter outfit."

So again we waited and again the doorman blew his whistle and again taxis rushed by and I was just about to say, "Oh, please let's walk, Father," when a taxi drew up and a man in top hat and tails bent forward and paid the driver and then went flying into the apartment house and my father pushed me into the taxi and climbed in after me.

Inside the taxi the floor was wet and the leather seats were slick and damp. I tucked one foot in my mother's silver shoe under me to try to get it warm. The street sounds rose up through the rain, the hissing of wheels on the wet streets and horns sounding impatient. Through the drenched windows I could see the people walking by, some with umbrellas radiating dangerous spikes—Luisa knows a girl who almost lost an eye when someone poked an umbrella spike into it—and women with newspapers over their heads and men holding umbrellas over their girls and getting soaked themselves.

We turned east and went down a dark side street where three little boys in leather jackets were trying to keep a bonfire going. A sheet of newspaper caught just as we went by and the flames rose up, bright and cheerful; I would have liked to get out of the taxi and go stand by the little boys instead of going on to dinner with my father. But then we crossed Third Avenue just as the el roared by overhead, and the taxi skidded a little on the old and unused trolley tracks so that for a moment I was afraid we were going to crash into one of the iron el posts. But my father held my arm tightly and then the taxi was across Third Avenue and the taxi driver turned around and grinned at us and said, "Almost scared myself that time."

I looked at his name under the picture and it was Hiram Schultz. Whenever I am in a taxi I always look to see if the man in the cab is the same one as the man in the picture. Hiram Schultz was the same and he did not seem to have any neck. His head went right down into his shoulders so that the collar of his red jacket came up to the tips of his ears.

The taxi stopped in front of a small basement restaurant. My mother and father eat a great deal in restaurants, but they don't often take me and I had never been in this one before. We walked by a small bar shaped like a half moon, and on into the back of the restaurant, which was long and narrow. Small tables lined the walls and there was just a narrow passageway between for the waiters.

"Well, Camilla," my father said, "this is the first time you've ever gone out to dinner alone with your old father, isn't it?"

"Yes, Father."

"And since you're a big girl now—fifteen, isn't it?— would you like to celebrate your maturity with one very small drink?"

"Yes, please, Father," I said, and then wished I hadn't, because I remembered Luisa warning me never to let anyone get me drunk. "*In vino veritas*, Camilla, *in vino veritas*," Luisa had told me, and since such sentiments were not taught in our Latin classes both of us were proud of being able to understand this. But since I had said I wanted a drink, I knew I would have to go through with it. My father is very formidable about people changing their minds, though my mother says it is a woman's privilege.

"What shall it be, Camilla?" my father asked. "I'm having a martini, but I'm afraid that wouldn't be a very good first choice for you."

I thought a minute and remembered a French movie Luisa and I had seen at the Fifth Avenue Playhouse where the heroine, who was quite young, went into a café to wait for someone. And she didn't know what to order, so the waiter suggested a vermouth cassis as being something fitting for a young girl. Luisa and I sat through the picture twice in order to memorize "vermouth cassis."

So I looked up at the waiter and said, "I'd like a vermouth cassis, please."

My father laughed. "Well, Camilla, am I wrong? This isn't your first drink?"

"Oh, yes," I said. "Except for the tastes of champagne."

The waiter put the martini in front of my father— pale liquid with a tiny twist of lemon peel, the color of my mother's hair—and the vermouth cassis in front of me. It was in a regular water glass with a little ice in it, and looked rather like a Coca-Cola without the fizz. I took a swallow, a very small one, because I remembered the movies where the heroine takes a big swallow of a drink, when it's her first one, and then gasps and coughs and tries to act as though she'd been drinking fire. The swallow did not burn me; it was both bitter and sweet at the same time and it tasted very warm all the way down. Most food stops tasting and feeling as soon as you swallow it, but I could feel the sip of vermouth cassis going down very warm, and somehow as comforting as sitting before an open fire on a cold night, all the way down to my stomach. I took another sip and it gave me the same lovely feeling, but I remembered Luisa saying "*In vino veritas*" and I remembered my mother's face all puckered up with fear and put my glass down and took a breadstick out of the little wicker basket in the center of the table.

The waiter did not bring us menus but stood hovering by my father's side and made suggestions in low intimate French that somehow reminded me of Jacques, although I have never heard Jacques speak anything but English. My father answered the waiter in French, but his French, instead of sounding all curves and music like Chopin or the ballet, was as square and angular as a problem in algebra. The waiter kept acting very pleased though, and when he went back out into the kitchen—where I had a glimpse of hot heavy air and copper saucepans hanging under a big copper hood, and a chef in a big white hat—my father laughed and said, "Camilla, my dear, you really must be growing up. I believe the waiter thinks I'm your sugar daddy."

I did not like it when my father said this. It made me think of a book of Peter Arno cartoons one of the girls at school, Alma Potter, keeps hidden in her desk. My father does not look in the least like one of Peter Arno's cartoons. But I could see that he thought he had made a very funny joke, so I laughed, too, because I wanted so terribly to keep the dark look out of his eyes. When my father gets the dark look in his eyes it is like the sky in summer when suddenly the daylight grows greeny black and you know it will be better when the thunder comes. Only with my father thunder does not come.

"Now I should offer you a mink coat and a diamond necklace," my father said, "but I am afraid those are a little beyond my means, even for my own darling girl. Would a couple of new books for those swelling bookcases of yours do as well?"

"Yes, thank you, Father," I said, "but you don't need to give me anything."

The waiter wheeled a little wagon up to us filled with trays of hors d'oeuvres. I was very hungry because I usually eat shortly after I come home from school, so I let him heap a little of everything on my plate.

"When a sugar daddy gives his baby a mink coat and a diamond necklace, he usually expects certain favors in return," my father said as the waiter wheeled the little table away. "What are you going to give me for those two promised books, Camilla?"

I looked at him rather blankly. "You know I haven't anything I could give you, Father," I said, and took a small nervous sip of my vermouth cassis. After all, even the Christmas and birthday presents I get for him are bought with the allowance money he gives me. I have never actually earned a penny of my own in my life.

"Well, you can give me your love, for one thing," he said, and began picking up lentils, one after the other, on one tine of his fork. "And your complete honesty is another thing I value. You've always been honest with your father, haven't you, Camilla?"

"Yes, Father," I said, and broke a breadstick in half so that small crumbs of it fell onto the rough white tablecloth.

"I would have liked more children," my father said then. "A son, maybe. But I am sure that no other child could ever give me the satisfaction and joy that you have."

My father had never spoken to me like this before. The only way I really knew that he loved me was that sometimes when I kissed him good night he would give me a rough hug that almost broke my ribs and sometimes he would bring me home a book that he had just happened to hear me mention I wanted, or a new map of the stars. "I love you very much, Camilla, do you know that?" he said now, and I wondered if this was *in vino veritas* and if it was because of his dry martini, which he had drunk very quickly and then followed with more.

I looked down at my plate and I had only eaten half the hors d'oeuvres and suddenly I couldn't eat any more and I took a big swallow of my vermouth cassis.

"Mademoiselle is finished?" the waiter asked, and took away my plate.

We had onion soup next. My father handed me a dish of Parmesan cheese and said, "Did you like the doll Jacques Nissen gave you?"

I sprinkled cheese over my soup. "No. I don't much care for dolls."

"What are you going to do with it?" my father asked.

"I'd like to give it to Luisa if that would be all right. She still likes dolls."

"Why not?" my father said. "It's yours to do as you please with."

The restaurant was filling up. People were crowded about the bar and sitting on the small uncomfortable chairs just inside the door. Occasionally the door would open, letting in a gust of dark rain-smelling air, and I would look at the door because somehow I could not look at my father.

The waiter took away my soup bowl and brought me a plate with stuffed mushrooms and tiny string beans and potatoes chopped up in cheese sauce. I tasted everything and then my father said, "Nissen comes to see you fairly often, Camilla. Do you like him?"

Luisa and I play a game called Indications, in which you have to guess a person by the things he reminds you of—colors and materials and animals and painters and things like that. And I did Jacques once for Luisa. I remember some of the things he reminded me of. For an animal it was a little stripy snake coiled around a rosebush; and the flower was the berry of the deadly nightshade and the painter was Daumier or Lautrec and the music was Debussy's "Golliwog's Cakewalk." And the weapon was a dagger or a poison ring and the method of transportation was a submarine and the drink was absinthe with lots of wormwood. I don't mean that Jacques is *like* these things, but when Luisa would ask me for instance what weapon does he remind you of, that was the kind of thing I had to answer. So what was I to say to my father?

I said, "Well, I don't really know him very well. He isn't very easy to talk to."

"But what does he talk to you about?" my father asked.

I took up my glass to take a sip of vermouth cassis and it was empty; there was only a little pale ice water in the bottom. I finished the ice water and it tasted stale and made me feel a little sick. I've never had a proper conversation with Jacques. When he is there I am in my room doing homework; sometimes I don't even go into the living room at all.

"Oh, well—I talk about school," I said. "Luisa and I almost got into awful trouble last week for something we did. Frank—he's Luisa's brother—was reading Plato and he found a sentence for us and we copied it and got to school early and hung it on the classroom door. It said, *All learning which is acquired under compulsion has no hold upon the mind.* When Miss Sargent came she said that it could be the work of nobody but Luisa Rowan and Camilla Dickinson and she kept us after school."

But my father did not want to change the subject as I had hoped that he might. He said, "Do you and Rose and Nissen have tea together?"

"Oh—sometimes," I said. I wanted to stick my fingers in my ears, partly to shut out my father's words and partly because my ears were buzzing and felt the way they sometimes do in the subway.

"Sometimes? What about the other times?"

"He really doesn't come so very often," I said.

"Is your mother usually in when you get home from school?"

How often does "usually" mean? Some days mother is home and some days she isn't and just hurries in a few minutes before time for my father to get home. So I really could say either that she's usually home or that she's usually out, so I said, "Usually, I guess." I pressed my cold fingers against my hot cheeks and prayed, Oh, make him stop. Please make him stop.

Then my father said, "Let's not beat around bushes anymore, Camilla. You're old enough to be asked a straight question. Does Nissen come to see you or does he come to see Rose?"

"I don't know," I said.

"You're not a fool, Camilla. Tell me the truth."

"I have to go to the ladies' room," I said. "I have to go quickly. I'm going to throw up." And I pushed my chair back in such a rush that it fell over and then I ran between the tables to the door marked LADIES and just reached the toilet in time to throw up. A big woman in a white uniform was sitting in a yellow satin chair knitting and she got up and held my head and then when I had finished she took a clean towel and wet it and washed my face and gave me some mouthwash and dashed my forehead with cologne. Then she put my head down against her bosom, which was very big and firm like an overblown air cushion, and said over and over, "You poor little thing, you poor little thing."

It was lovely there with my face pressed against the

top button of her white uniform and her big hand rubbing gently in between my shoulder blades. I would have liked to stay there but I said, "My father will be worried. I'm all right, now. Thank you very much."

The woman released me and I took my head away from her nice clean uniform and looked up at her and said "Thank you" again. Her face was covered with lots of white powder and underneath the powder it was as full of freckles as the Milky Way is full of stars.

"Fancy letting a baby like you have anything to drink," she said. "Your father, is it? He ought to know better. Sure you're all right now, pet?"

"Yes, thank you," I told her. "You've been awfully nice to me." I would have liked to ask her what her name was; I would have liked somehow to see her again because she was as comforting as a mountain; but I just shook hands with her and went out into the restaurant again.

When I got back to the table my father was very worried and very sweet to me and he paid the bill and we left the restaurant. Outside it had stopped raining and turned much colder. Clouds were breaking up and racing across the sky, and the sidewalk had almost dried except for where it was uneven and the puddles lay like dark shadows in the night.

"Shall we get a taxi or would it make you feel better to walk a little?" my father asked.

"Let's walk," I said. The black shocking air felt

wonderful to my hot cheeks. I looked up and through a big rip in the clouds I saw a star; and I wished. Luisa thinks it is terrible for me to wish on stars, but I know she wishes on them herself; and I like to do it even though it isn't scientific. I think that it is good to believe in things like wishing on stars but bad to believe in things like black cats crossing your path and seeing the new moon through glass. I like wishbones, too, and wishing on the first bite of a birthday cake; and Luisa and I have always said "bread and butter" when a lamppost or anything goes between us, though I'm not sure that that is as constructive a superstition as the others.

"Did you know that there are meteoric showers in winter?" I asked my father. "There are the Ursids and the Epsilon Arietids and the Orionids. And there are the Taurids and the Andromedids. Aren't those beautiful words, Father?"

"Yes," my father said, and all the rest of the way home we did not say another word. But he held my hand in his—we both had our gloves in our pockets in spite of the cold wind—and every once in a while my father would press my hand with his strong fingers. We walked up Second Avenue for a while and then we turned west toward Third, and again an el train went by with the lights warmly yellow in the windows; it looked as though everybody inside must be comfortable and companionable and perhaps even talking together to help keep the night out of the train. But

I knew that in reality they were probably tired and cross and in a hurry to get home and change into dry slippers; or perhaps some of them might have no place to go except a flophouse, or not even a quarter for that, and were waiting for a chance to spread out a newspaper on one of the seats and sleep there.

When we got to the apartment my father asked, "Do you feel better, dear?"

"Yes," I said. But I did not want to go into the house. I wanted my father to go in and leave me outside to walk and walk out on the streets and maybe go into Central Park and sit down on a bench and talk to someone else who wanted to be out all night walking too.

But my father pressed my hand again and we went upstairs. We went into the living room; it was dark there, but my father did not turn on the lights. We walked over to the window and stood looking out. From the living-room windows you can see across Central Park to the apartments on Central Park West and you can see Radio City and Essex House and Hampshire House and the tip of the Empire State Building and it is all more beautiful even than pictures of the Rocky Mountains and the Grand Canyon.

"Camilla," my father said, "Camilla, I was mad or drunk or both. I shouldn't have—" and then he didn't say anything more.

I waited awhile and he just stood there beside me and held my hand so tightly that I could feel my bones creaking together, and at last I said, "It's all right, Father."

"Is it, Camilla?" he asked.

"Yes," I said, and I tried to make my voice sound very firm.

My father let my hand go then and said, "Let's go see if your mother is awake."

We walked very softly to my mother's room. It is my father's room, too, in that he sleeps there, but the room that we call his room is his study, where he sometimes works after he's come home from the office and where he usually goes to read his paper. The light in my mother's room was on and she was still on the chaise longue, but she was sound asleep with her hair falling over the pillow and one hand drooping over the side so that it almost touched the floor; she looked as lovely and innocent and helpless as the princess in "The Sleeping Beauty."

"I'm going to do some homework now and go to bed," I whispered to my father, standing just on the threshold of the room where my mother lay so exquisitely asleep. "Good night, Father."

"Good night, Camilla," he whispered back, but he did not look at me. He kept on looking at my mother.

I did homework until I was sleepy and then I got ready for bed. I did everything rather numbly, because I didn't want to let myself think. I had just opened the window and turned out the light when there was a soft knock and the door opened and my mother stood there outlined in the light from the hall.

"Are you asleep, darling?" she whispered.

"No."

She came in and sat down beside me on the bed and began stroking my forehead gently, the way she used to sometimes when I was very small and was in bed with a fever.

"Did you have a nice dinner with your father?"

"Yes, thank you."

"Did he—what did you talk about?"

"Oh—I don't know—the dinner."

"Did he ask you—was there— Did he mention Jacques?"

"He asked me if I liked the doll."

My mother kept on stroking my forehead and suddenly she bent down and leaned over me as though she were trying to protect me from something, and whispered, "Oh, Camilla, oh, my darling baby, I do love you so much."

"I love you, too, Mother," I said. "I love you terribly." And suddenly I wanted to cry, but I knew that I must not.

My mother sat up again and continued her stroking of my forehead. When I was a small child, the soothing repetitive motion used to lull me to sleep, but now it seemed to make me wide-awake and tense, and it was my mother's voice as she spoke that sounded sleepy.

"Most people don't realize that love can be killed,"

she said in a soft drowsy voice. "When someone tells you he loves you, you don't expect him to reject it when you offer him your love in return."

I lay rigid in bed and the cold air from the open window blew against my hot cheeks and my mother in her rose velvet gown shivered. "You really do love me, darling, you really do?" she asked.

"I love you, Mother," I said, and I had to close my eyelids down very tightly to keep the tears inside.

"I wish—" she said softly, "I wish Mama were alive. I wish I had somebody to talk to. Tod, or even Jen." Uncle Tod and Aunt Jen were her brother and sister, who lived far away from New York. "I wish— Mama used to worry about me. She always thought I was a fool in a—in a nice sort of way." Then she let out a long shivering sigh. "Are you happy, darling?" she asked me. "Is everything all right? Are you happy at school?"

"Yes, Mother," I said.

"Are you sleepy?"

"Yes."

"You're not—you're not worried about anything?"

"No, Mother."

"That's all right, then. I thought you seemed—I thought maybe something had happened to make you upset at school."

"No. Everything's fine at school," I said.

2

Thursday morning I had not quite finished getting dressed when the telephone rang and it was Luisa saying, "Camilla, let's have breakfast together at a drugstore, *please?*" Her voice quivered with urgency.

"Okay, where?" I asked, and I was glad that she had called. My mother usually has breakfast in bed, but my father and I eat breakfast together, and I felt that it would be easier for me to talk to him if I didn't have to see him till evening.

My mother came out of the bedroom just as I was putting on my hat and coat. "Camilla, where are you going?" she demanded. She did not look like the Sleeping Beauty or a princess in a fairy tale this morning. Her face looked white and all the lines in it were dragged down by tiredness and anxiety and other things I was not able to read, and she held her dressing gown around her as though she were cold.

"I'm going to meet Luisa for breakfast."

"For breakfast! Why?"

"I think she's—disturbed—about something," I said.

"Are you—are you all right, darling?" my mother asked.

"Yes, thank you."

"Are you—are you coming right home after school?"

"I don't know," I said. "I guess so."

"But you won't be late?"

"No," I said. "I have to go now, Mother. I promised Luisa I'd meet her right away."

I kissed my mother and left, and I felt terribly isolated and the way I imagine a stranger in a foreign country would feel, because I did not know what to say to either my mother or my father. Talking to them had become like talking to strangers, where you have to search wildly for something casual and unimportant to say.

I took Jacques's doll with me and left it in the coatroom at school for Luisa, because I couldn't bear to leave anything at home that would remind me so continually of Jacques. I used to pray desperately that he would not come to our apartment. Now I did not ask for quite as much; I asked simply that my father should never come home early and see Jacques with my mother again. And then I wondered: Why did Father come home early yesterday afternoon?

So I left the doll in the coatroom for Luisa and went

to the drugstore around the corner where she was waiting for me. There was a cup of coffee and a glass of orange juice, almost exactly the color of her hair, on the counter before her. "I'm so upset I can't possibly eat another thing for breakfast," she exclaimed as I climbed up on the stool beside her. "Anyhow, I'm broke."

"I can lend you fifty cents," I said. "What's the matter?"

"Oh, *them* again, of course, Mona and Bill." Luisa always called her parents by their first names.

"What now?" I asked.

"Oh, they had a fight last night when they came in. At first they tried to whisper so Frank and I wouldn't hear, and they whispered louder and louder and finally they yelled and Mona ended up throwing a whole Beethoven symphony at my father, record by record. From the number of crashes it sounded like the Ninth."

She took a big swallow of coffee and then made a face. Luisa's mouth moves more than any other mouth I have ever seen when she talks or even when she just listens. Whenever I try to describe it, it sounds ugly and perhaps taken by itself it would be, but in her face it doesn't give the effect of being ugly at all. It is a long mouth, almost as though someone had taken a knife and made a slash across her face; and the lips are narrow but because they are so flexible you don't get any impression of thinness or sharpness. Frank calls Luisa ugly, but the thing I like about her face is that it is like a windy morning with lots of clouds moving rapidly across the sky, all lights and shadows; and though she has red hair her eyes are not green like mine, but are like bright chinks of blue. And her face is very white, with as many freckles as the woman in the ladies' room of the restaurant.

"I don't see why they couldn't have had their fight before they came home," Luisa said. "The worst part was when people stuck their heads out of windows and told them to shut up." She finished her orange juice, holding the glass very tight with one of her nice bony hands. Her hands are very strong; she can open the tightest bottle of ink. "How're yours?" she asked me.

"Oh—all right, I guess," I said.

"That means all wrong," Luisa said. "Can you really lend me fifty cents, Camilla?"

"Sure."

"But you know I can't pay it back."

"Oh—someday when we're both famous you will." I get twice the allowance Luisa gets—or twice the amount she's supposed to get. Sometimes I don't think she really gets any.

"I'll have a minced ham sandwich," Luisa said. "What's yours, Camilla?"

"Lettuce, tomato, and bacon." A nice thing about Luisa and me—we both like sandwiches for breakfast and we like cereal before we go to bed at night.

"I suppose that Jacques Nissen was there yesterday," Luisa said.

"Yes." The funny thing is that even before I told

Luisa anything about how I feel about Jacques, when he first started coming, she knew just how I felt and she knows every time I have come home from school and found him there.

"You know," Luisa said, pouring sugar into her coffee, "you've changed a lot since we've known each other."

"Have I?"

"Yes. Matured. I mean about Them. It's a funny thing, Camilla. I always thought I couldn't bear it if anything bad happened to you, but I feel ever so much closer to you just because of your mother and Jacques and your being unhappy and everything."

"Oh," I said. I told the man who was making our sandwiches, "I'd like a chocolate milkshake too," and then I just sat there with my elbows on the counter and remembered when I first met Luisa over a year ago. She came into school about three weeks late. Her parents were having a vacation on Fire Island and they just didn't bother to come back to New York in time for Luisa to get to school. I didn't have much of a chance to talk to her the first week; she wasn't shy and everybody liked her right away and she always seemed to be with a group of people. But one afternoon when I went over to the Metropolitan Museum I met her.

Last year was my first year without a governess, the first year I was allowed to go to school or anywhere I wanted to alone; and sometimes I used to take my books over to the museum and study. My mother hadn't met Jacques then so it wasn't because of that; it was just that it was the first chance I'd ever had to be really by myself. Anyhow the museum with its enormous echoing rooms and great glassed roofs has always been one of my favorite places. When I was little and Binny, my nurse, used to take me to the park to play, I always made her walk with me through the museum. I loved the Egyptian tombs especially, and the mummies; and I loved the great halls hung with embroidered flags and shields and swords and filled with suits of armor in which I liked to imagine real little knights. How tiny men must have been in those days; my father couldn't anywhere nearly get into the largest of the suits of armor. Maybe Jacques could, but it would be a tight pinch even for him. Somehow, and this is a strange thing, I can imagine both my father and Jacques being knights riding off to the Crusades with their ladies' handkerchiefs as a talisman: it's the only way I can imagine both my father and Jacques at the same time.

The particular afternoon when I first got to know Luisa I went to a room that is like the courtyard of a Roman house, with a marble pool in the center, and marble benches at the sides. It has trees and plants and the warm moist odor of a greenhouse. I sat down on one of the benches and opened my history book and I felt very happy because the history we were studying then was Roman history and it was a wonderful place to do it in. After a while someone sat down beside me and said "Hello" and it was Luisa. I wasn't particularly glad to see her just then (though I had been wanting a chance to get to know her at school) because I was happy by myself and I wanted to do my history, but she kept on sitting there, so we talked. At first we didn't talk much about anything, just about school and the girls and the teachers. Then she said, "You know what, Camilla Dickinson? I've been thinking and I've decided that I like you better than anyone else in school."

I didn't know what to say to this. I never could have said anything like that to anyone, no matter how much I meant it, but it sounded all right the way she said it, looking straight at me with her blue eyes alive and friendly; and suddenly it made me very happy. She looked at me and I looked at her and I couldn't say anything and then out of a blue sky she asked me, "Do you love your mother and father?"

"Of course," I said.

She shook her head impatiently so that her straight red hair flopped back and forth across her cheeks. "I don't mean the 'of course' kind of love. I don't mean do you love them for being your mother and father. I mean do you love them as people?"

I'd never thought of Mother and Father, then, as being anything but Mother and Father. I mulled her words over in my mind for a moment, and then I answered "Yes."

"You're very lucky," Luisa said. "I don't like either of mine."

This was something I couldn't imagine, and I must

have looked very blank and stupid because Luisa twisted her mouth into a sad sort of smile and then she asked me if I had any brothers and sisters and I told her that I hadn't.

"Do you think your parents wanted you to be born?" Luisa asked. I looked blank and stupid again, and Luisa went on. "My dear child, don't you realize that lots of times parents don't want their children at all? Frank and I were planned but I think it was a great mistake. Were you planned?"

"I don't know," I said.

Luisa sighed. She sat there on the marble bench and put her elbows on her knees and her chin on her hands and looked as though she might at any moment burst into tears. "You're very lucky," Luisa said. "You're one of these people who's a daughter and your mother and father are parents; but Frank and I and my mother and father are all separate people and we're in eternal conflict. Do you know, Camilla Dickinson, you're the kind of person it's easy to talk to. I don't ever talk to people like this. Would you be my friend? I do so need to have a real friend."

Luisa puzzled me and she frightened me a little, but I wanted very much to be her friend, if, after this talk, she didn't think I was too stupid. "I'd like to be your friend," I said.

She lifted her chin from her hands and her face changed from being all tight with trying not to cry and lit up with a smile. "Then it's all settled!" she shouted, and shook my hand.

After that we did our homework together almost every afternoon, either at her apartment on Ninth Street or up at mine. Her parents weren't around often and Frank was away at boarding school that winter, so we had her apartment pretty much to ourselves. It's quite a small apartment—the third-floor-through of a brownstone house; it has a big living room with two studio couches where her parents sleep and a long blond wood table where they all eat and a kitchenette in a closet; and in the back are two small bedrooms where Frank and Luisa sleep with a bath between. Luisa's room has a double-decker bed. The room isn't big enough for two beds except one on top of the other, and she and Frank both used to sleep in this room when they were very little.

Luisa's apartment has a very different feel from mine. In her living room all the furniture is very modern-looking; the chairs are oddly shaped and much more comfortable than you'd expect them to be, though rather hard to get out of. There are very modern paintings on the walls, most of them originals, because Luisa's mother works on an art magazine. I wish I could explain the mood of that apartment. Whenever I am there I feel that life is very dangerous and exciting and that I am rather dull and unprepared for it. I don't feel uncomfortable in it because Luisa is somehow part of it, and I never feel uncomfortable with Luisa; but until this year it has been something very far removed from my life.

"Camilla, stop brooding," Luisa said, finishing her

minced ham sandwich and licking her fingers. "Did you talk to Jacques yesterday?"

"Yes. He brought me a doll."

"A doll! To you! Beware of the Greeks bearing gifts, Camilla. What does he think you are! What an insult! I hope you threw it in his face!" Luisa got very excited and banged on the counter with her fist so that the sleeve of her yellow sweater pulled up above her narrow wrist and made her suddenly seem to me younger than I am. Luisa is a year older than I and usually she seems much older but every once in a while I feel as old as one of the burned-out mountains of the moon and Luisa is like a little comet flinging itself violently across the sky.

"I brought the doll for you," I said. "I left it in the coatroom at school. It's in a box. It's really a lovely one—as dolls go."

"For me!" Luisa looked up at the counterman and smiled at him radiantly. "Oh, Camilla, really! You are a darling! Do you think I'm an awful dope, still liking dolls? You'll never tell any of the kids at school, will you? What a thing Alma Potter'd make of it! Thank goodness it's in a box. It doesn't look like a doll, does it? The box, I mean?"

"No," I assured her.

"Frank thinks I'm a dope," she said. "My gosh, I wish Frank were back at boarding school this year. But I guess even if he hadn't been kicked out last winter Mona and Bill couldn't have sent him back this year. You don't know, Camilla, but really he's impossible to live with. It's hell being poor, absolute hell. I don't know why Mona and Bill don't send me to public school too. A batty sort of pride when half the time we don't have enough to eat. Listen, Camilla, you won't ever think I'm a dope, will you?"

"Of course not," I said.

Luisa finished her coffee and I finished my milk-shake, sucking on my straws gently so that I'd get all of it without making that bubbly sucking noise too loudly.

"Come on," Luisa said. "Let's go to school."

The day after I'd met Luisa in the Roman courtyard at the museum last year I came right home from school. My mother was shopping and I went into the kitchen and got some milk and bread and sugar and went into my room to do homework. In just a few minutes the doorbell rang and it was Luisa. "Hello, Luisa," I said. "Come on in my room and help me with Latin. I'm having an awful time."

Luisa stood there just inside the door and pulled off her yellow string gloves and twisted them. "Are you sure your mother won't mind my coming?"

"Of course not," I said. "She's out anyhow."

"Oh," Luisa said, and her mouth drooped with disappointment. "I wanted to see her."

"Well, she'll probably be back soon," I said. "Did you want to see her about anything particular?"

Luisa shook her head and her eyes wandered about the hall, pausing at the mahogany table with the silver tray for calling cards and the two mahogany chairs with yellow brocade seats and the beautiful map on the wall—a map of America made long ago when most of the continent was unknown territory. "I just wanted to see what kind of mother you would have," she said.

"Well, come on in my room," I told her. She followed me in and stood looking around there, too, still twisting her gloves in her nice bony fingers. Luisa is very thin; she is even thinner than I am.

"Camilla," Luisa said, "your mother is wonderful, isn't she?"

"Yes."

"She understands things, doesn't she? You can talk to her."

"Yes." Because I could, then. I could talk to Mother about anything, although when I was little it was always Father who gave me a sense of strength and security. It was as though Mother and I were sisters who played all kinds of wonderful games together, but Father was the parent who had the power to make things all right.

Luisa threw her gloves on my bed and scowled down at my pillow and said, "I don't want to go home. I don't want go back there tonight."

"Do you want to spend the night with me?" I asked.

"Don't be silly," Luisa said. "That wouldn't be any good. Things have come to a pretty pass, haven't they, when I have to say I don't want to go back, ever ever ever!" She said each "ever" louder, and on

44

the last one she took off her hat and threw it on the floor. "I'm so unhappy!" she said.

I sat down at the foot of my bed and my room seemed suddenly full of something it had never contained before. I had cried there, had even had tantrums there when I was very little, but the room had never seemed full to the point of explosion the way it did now with Luisa jerking off her plaid scarf, her brown tweed coat, and stamping and shaking her head to keep from bursting into tears.

"It was a bad day for you, Camilla Dickinson, when you said you'd be my friend," she said in a harsh voice. "I'll drag you through the depths with me. All our family are like that. We're terrible to our friends. But we do care about them. We love them. Truly we do." For a moment her lips quivered and she turned away so that I could not see her face.

"They're being polite, now," she said. "Mona and Bill. My mother and father. It's worst of all when they're polite. When they shout and throw things it's bad, but it's not nearly as bad because when they care enough about each other to slap and hit and scream, they really must love each other, don't you think? Frank and I have terrible fights, but if he died I think I'd die too. But when they're polite, then I really get frightened. Camilla, I'm so afraid they'll get a divorce. And what do you suppose would happen to Frank and me if they did? Bill would probably take Frank and Mona would take me, and I like Bill better than Mona even if he is awful to her. Anyhow, it's better being together just anyhow than it would be to be separated. Why don't you say something?"

I sat there at the foot of my bed and I didn't know what to say. I thought that Luisa would hate me and would never bother with me again because I was so stupid. I wanted terribly to say something that would be wise and strong, and then I knew with finality that there was nothing for me to say, nothing at all.

Then we heard the front door slam and my mother came running down the hall to my room, crying, "Camilla darling, where are you?" She came bursting into my room and stopped short when she saw Luisa. She smiled at Luisa as though she were terribly pleased to see her, and said, "Why, hello!"

"This is Luisa Rowan, Mother," I said. "Luisa, this is my mother."

My mother smiled at Luisa again and dumped a big box on my bed. "Darling, I brought you two new skirts and two new—I was passing a shop and there they were in the window so I went—the sweaters are lovely, Camilla, cashmere and wonderful colors. Do try them on."

So I had to open the box and try on the clothes while Luisa sat there and watched me and her blue eyes seemed to grow dark and I could not tell whether it was with hate or envy or sorrow. My mother made me leave on one of the sweaters and skirts and then she said, "Darling, Raff and I are going out to dinner and the theater tonight with some friends. Don't you want your friend to— Would you like to keep Camilla company for supper, Luisa?"

"Yes, thank you," Luisa said very quietly. "I'd like to very much."

Luisa was quiet all the rest of the evening. She didn't say anything else violent and all of a sudden she seemed as happy and comfortable as a kitten.

The day after Luisa first came to our apartment, we were having milk and cookies at recess, and she asked me, "Camilla, what are you going to be?"

"You mean when I grow up?" I asked.

"Now, there you go again, Camilla," Luisa said. "You're grown-up right now to all intents and purposes. When you're old enough to be on your own, to do what you want to do, I mean."

"An astronomer," I said. I threw the word at her as though it were a stone because I was afraid she would laugh at me.

And she did. She said, "Oh, Camilla, people go to psychiatrists now, not astronomers. Astronomers are outmoded nowadays. Anyhow, you'd never be any good at telling fortunes and things because you don't know anything about people."

Now it was my turn to laugh. It was the first time I'd ever laughed *at* Luisa instead of along with her. "You're thinking of an astrologer," I said. "I mean a real astronomer, a scientist, the kind they have at Palomar."

"Oh," Luisa said. She pulled on her straws until she

had finished her chocolate milk and then she asked, "Why?" But there was for the first time real respect in her voice.

"I don't know exactly," I said. "It's just something I've always wanted. My Grandmother Wilding used to teach me about stars. She knew an awful lot. She'd even met and talked to Maria Mitchell."

"Who's Maria Mitchell?"

"One of the first women astronomers. Oh, Luisa, doesn't it give you a shivery sort of feeling at night when you look up in the sky and half the stars you see aren't there anymore? Or at any rate they're dead and they haven't had any light on them for thousands of years. It takes light so long to travel all that distance that we're seeing them as they were thousands of years ago. And listen. What does the name Schiaparelli mean to you?" Now I was showing off and I knew it, but I didn't care. I did well in school, but she was the one who always seemed to know about outside things.

"Schiaparelli? A famous dress designer, of course. Any dope knows that. Why?"

"Well," I said, "to me it means Giovanni Virginio Schiaparelli, an Italian astronomer—he came from Milan, as a matter of fact—in the nineteenth century."

"Okay, okay," Luisa said. "So what did this guy do?"

"Well," I told her, "for one thing he was the first astronomer to see the canals on Mars. Oh—and he was the first one to discover that Mercury takes eighty-eight days to rotate."

"Okay, okay," Luisa said again. "I'm convinced. You're going to be an astronomer."

"I am."

Luisa grinned at me. "But you take your Schiaparelli and I'll take mine. Maybe if my clothes came from Schiaparelli instead of bargain basements I wouldn't look so bony."

I laughed then and said, "I didn't mean to get so excited. But, oh, Luisa, it's so terribly exciting! Did you know that some scientists think that the world and the sun and the planets and lots of the other stars are all part of a great big explosion? A huge enormous star exploded somewhere and we're all just fragments of that explosion getting farther and farther apart as we fly out into space."

"Don't," Luisa said. "That's scary."

"I think it's thrilling," I said. "You'd think it would be the religious people who'd want to find out about it all, wouldn't you? But most of them don't. What do you want to be, Luisa?"

"A doctor," Luisa said. "Either a psychiatrist or a surgeon. I'd like to be a psychiatrist because I'd like to know what makes people throw things at each other and hate each other and love each other at the same time; and drink too much; and cry all night long. And I'd like to be a surgeon because it would be a lot of really complicated problems, much harder than algebra or geometry, and I'm not a bit afraid of blood and gore and I think lots of doctors cut up an awful lot more of people than needs to be cut up. And it would be terribly exciting to be a surgeon, too, don't you think, Camilla?"

"Yes," I said, "I guess it would," and in my mind's ear I could hear Luisa being talked about as "that brilliant woman surgeon, Luisa Rowan," and I could see her walking into the operating room and putting rubber gloves on her long bony fingers with quick decisive gestures and then afterward looking terribly white and exhausted and at the same time terribly pleased. . . .

"And it's nice," Luisa said, "our both wanting to be scientists. Do let's always be friends, Camilla, even when you're a famous astronomer and I'm a famous doctor. Maybe neither of us will ever get married and then we'll need to be friends more than ever. I don't think I'll ever get married. I'm ugly and I'm flat-chested and I'm darned if I'll buy any of those little rubber things you stick in your bra. And I don't like men anyhow. Frank always goes around brooding and Bill is horrible to Mona even if I do like him better. I don't like women, either, I guess. Maybe I'm a misogynist. Is that what I mean? Or is it misanthrope? Anyhow, I don't think I'll ever get married unless I find a doctor who's a misogynist too. And you'll have your career to think of. You'll probably have lots of violent love affairs but a marriage might interfere with your work. Scientists should be single-minded. I really agree with Mona and Bill when they say that marriage is outmoded."

"Well, I'd like—" I started, but she didn't even hear me.

"So we'll just have to go on being friends more than ever. And if you get ill or have any horrible accidents or anything I'll take care of you and save your life. Or maybe I could psychoanalyze you. Golly, Camilla, maybe it would be good if I psychoanalyzed you right now!"

Fortunately, the bell for the end of recess rang then and we crammed the rest of our cookies into our mouths and went back to the classroom.

I don't know what I'd have done without Luisa when Jacques started coming to see Mother. But knowing Luisa and having met Mona and Bill had somehow blunted the first edge of shock, though nothing could really prepare me for the fact that something like Jacques could happen to my own parents. It was like accidents in newspapers that always happen to someone else and then all of a sudden someone else is you.

On Thursday—the afternoon of the day after I saw Jacques and my mother kissing and I knew that I could no longer pretend that Jacques really wasn't important—I came straight home from school after all because Luisa was going to the movies with Frank. They asked me to go with them, but it was to a revival of a Boris Karloff horror picture on Forty-second Street and they always terrify me.

When I got home I could tell from the doorman and the elevator boy that Jacques was not there.

Upstairs the apartment was very quiet. I could hear Carter and the new cook talking out in the kitchen and I thought that perhaps my mother was out with Jacques. That was bad but it wasn't as bad as having Jacques in the apartment. I went out to the kitchen for a glass of milk, and Carter and the cook stopped suddenly as I appeared. The new cook seems very nice; at any rate I like her better than Carter. Carter is like a fish. I think if you cut her open her blood, like a fish's, would run cold.

"Is Mother out?" I asked, and then wished I hadn't asked it.

But Carter said, "No, Miss Camilla. I think she's in her room."

If Mother is home and not in the living room with Jacques she usually comes hurrying to meet me when I get back from school, and we have tea together, or cocoa, and talk; so I gulped down my milk and went to her room and knocked on the door.

There wasn't any answer, but just as I raised my hand to knock again, my mother's voice called, "Who is it?" Her voice sounded thick and as though she were talking through a bad cold.

"It's me, Mother," I said. "Camilla."

"Oh," my mother said. "Come in, darling. I think I'm catching a cold."

But when I went into the room and looked at her I knew she was not catching cold. She lay in a little heap on the bed with all her clothes, even her shoes, still on, and her face was all blurred and blotchy and looked as though she had been crying for hours and hours, the way Luisa says Mona does.

"Camilla darling," my mother said. "Be a sweet angel and throw my blanket over me, I'm freezing. Winter's really here, isn't it? I hate to see summer over and even autumn—though there were some nice warm days in October. I do hate the cold. How was school? Did you have a nice breakfast with Luisa?"

"Yes, thank you," I said.

"Camilla, come here, come here quick," my mother said, holding her arms out to me. I went over to the bed and she put her arms around me and pulled me down beside her and I could feel her tears spilling over onto my cheeks. "Oh, Camilla, don't hate me. Don't hate me too much," my mother wept.

"I don't hate you," I said quickly, and I kissed her with little gentle kisses as though she were the baby and I the mother; but for the first time as she lay there and wept she looked much older than I, really old enough to be my mother.

One thing that always pleases her when we go out someplace together is when people think we are sisters, or say, "And which is the mother and which is the daughter?" But now she had deep blue circles spreading out under her eyes like fans and her face seemed somehow to have puffed and sagged and I wanted to take her into my arms and hold her against me to protect her so that she would not see her face in the mirror.

"Oh, Mother, I love you," I said over and over. "I love you so much." And we clung together and rocked back and forth until at last my mother stopped crying and lay back against the pillows again, gasping and hiccuping like an exhausted baby. I went into her bathroom and wrung out her washcloth in cold water and bathed her eyes, and then I took some of her eau de cologne from her dressing table and rubbed it gently over her forehead, and she lay there with her eyes closed, saying, "Oh, that feels so good, Camilla, that feels so wonderful," and I felt old.

And then she said, "Oh, darling, I know I'm not very mature, but how can you please a person when you seem to be the very opposite of everything he wants? I don't have a brilliant mind the way he— All I have to offer him is my love. And when it seems to me he doesn't want—when he congratulates me because I'm less loving—oh, he doesn't use those words, of course, he calls it being more mature, but that's what it means —then it's as though he thrusts a knife in my— Once he even congratulated me on being more cold—to *him*. That hurt me more than— But I love him. I—I even tried to be less affectionate—but I couldn't kill the need for warmth that's in me."

She stopped talking then, with a sort of little gasp, and put her hand up to her mouth in a quick, childish gesture. Then she added in a whisper, "If only I had Mama to talk to—but I have to talk to someone. I can't help it, I've always had to talk. If only one didn't have to grow up, Camilla! If only one could always be a child! I'm not strong enough for—oh, Camilla, God help me, God help me!" And she began to cry again, and through her crying she said, "He'd murder me if he ever really knew—he'd murder me—Rafferty's a violent man, Camilla, you don't know how violent!"

"Why would Father want to murder you, Mother?" I asked, and my voice was suddenly as cold and as hard as a slab of marble.

She stopped crying suddenly then and sat up and held out both her hands to me. "Oh, dear God, Camilla, what have I done to you? What have I said? Of course he wouldn't want to murder—I'm just hysterical. I'm getting the flu and I don't know what I'm talking about. Call for the doctor, Camilla. I want to see Doctor Wallace. Call him for me."

I called the doctor and he said he would come by later in the evening; and I wanted to ask my mother, "Does everything you've been saying mean you love Jacques now and not Father?" And I wanted to say "How can you love that horrible little slug?" But I just covered her up with the blanket again and left the room and closed the door quietly behind me.

I went into my room and I did my homework. I forced my mind into a vacuum and then I filled that vacuum with the things I was supposed to learn or prepare for school the next day. I had never done my homework so quickly before. Then I went into the kitchen and told the new cook that I had been invited to have dinner with Luisa and I was sorry I hadn't mentioned it to her before. I am not supposed to go out in the evenings alone and Carter knows this, but she didn't say anything, and I went downstairs and walked to the BMT. I didn't know whether Luisa would have come home from the movies yet or not, but I thought I would go down to Ninth Street and see; and if worse came to worst I could go to a movie myself and then to her apartment afterward.

Someone was home when I rang the bell under the Rowan mailbox because the latch of the red front door clicked almost immediately. I pushed the door open and began to climb the brown carpeted stairs and from above I could hear Mona's English bulldog, Oscar Wilde, barking ferociously. As I started the last flight Mona leaned over the stair rail and called down, "Who is it?" and Oscar stuck his head through the banisters and growled. Oscar always looks as though he intends to eat you up when in reality all he wants is to sit in your lap and have his head scratched.

"It's Camilla Dickinson, Mrs. Rowan," I said. "Is Luisa home?"

Mona is very small and very thin with red hair cut almost as short as a man's, and she wears glasses with heavy black frames, and black suits and spike heels and hats from Lilly Daché, and I am always uncomfortable around her. When I go down to Luisa's I'm always glad when Mona isn't home because I feel that she thinks Luisa's friends are a bore and a nuisance, cluttering up her apartment.

"No, Luisa isn't home," she said. "Why didn't you call before coming all this distance?"

"Oh, I was coming down here anyhow." I lied for no reason except that, as usual, she rattled me so,

I didn't know what I was saying. "Tell Luisa I'll call her later." Now Oscar began to announce with an even louder voice that he wanted to see me, and he began jumping up and down and yipping with excitement between his barks. "Get inside and shut up, Oscar," Mona said, and, taking him by the collar, she flung him into the apartment. "I'll tell Luisa," she said, and slammed the door.

Well, I suppose I'll have to go to a movie, I thought, and I didn't like the idea because I'd never been to a movie alone. I turned around and had started down the stairs again when the door of the Rowan apartment opened and Frank stuck his head out, shouting, "Hey, Camilla Dickinson, is that you?" and came pounding down the stairs after me.

"Oh, hello, I thought you were at the movies with Luisa," I said. Frank made me feel uncomfortable, though in a different way from Mona, and I didn't know why. Perhaps it was just because he was a boy and I didn't know much about boys except the ones at dancing school, and I didn't like them.

"I got bored, so I came out early. Where are you going now?"

"I don't know. Just for a walk, I guess." My voice trailed off as I thought of having left my mother there, worn out on the bed from weeping, waiting for Father and Dr. Wallace to come and make everything all right. I thought that perhaps I should go home and then I thought that it might be better if Father came home and could be alone with Mother.

"Why don't I walk with you for a while?" Frank asked.

"Do you want to?"

"Yes. I'd like to see you once without Luisa."

As we started to walk, the streetlamps came on suddenly and the early winter night seemed to settle down between the houses.

"Where shall we go?" Frank asked.

"I don't care. Wherever you say," I said.

We walked over to Washington Square; above the arch we could see the first star pulsing and throbbing against the last cold streaks of light.

Washington Square has always seemed to me to be a much more grown-up park than Central Park. Perhaps it's because I used to play in Central Park when I was small and I've only really known Washington Square after dark when Luisa and I have walked Oscar Wilde around and around and talked. I felt very grown-up walking with Frank and almost as though I were an NYU student on a date. The park was emptying as we reached it. A few remaining mothers rolled up their knitting or closed their books with cold fingers and started pushing their baby carriages toward home, and a gang of boys was still bouncing a ball against the hard stone of the arch and shouting at each other with harsh, hungry voices.

"You know, Cam," Frank said, "Luisa monopolizes you. You shouldn't let her do that."

"She doesn't monopolize me," I said.

Frank picked a stick up off the sidewalk and threw it across the grass. "I suppose we should have brought Oscar Wilde with us. That dog would never get out if Luisa and I didn't see to him. Of course she monopolizes you. And you do whatever she tells you to do, meek as Oscar when he's chewed up one of Bill's shoes. And the funny thing is, I bet you've really got more guts than Luisa. Listen, Camilla Dickinson, do you believe in God?"

Frank looks very much like Luisa. His hair is a darker shade of red, but he has the same blue eyes and long arms with the naked wristbones always showing below his sweater and making him look younger than he is. And I saw now that he talked like Luisa, too, because that was the kind of question Luisa was apt to ask anybody new who interested her. She asks that sort of question partly because it shocks people and partly because she doesn't believe in God and she really wants to know what other people think. I think perhaps she feels that if she finds enough people who really believe in God, maybe she'll believe in Him again too.

It's the only thing we've ever really fought about—I mean a real fight, not just a spat. Luisa has to have a spat at least once a day. But about this all she'll ever say is "You're just a dope to believe in God, Camilla," with such scorn that I seem to shrivel and curl all up inside though I am determined to go on being a dope if that makes me a dope.

So now I said "Yes!" to Frank almost as though he had raised a whip over my head.

"That's very refreshing," Frank said, "very refreshing indeed. Do you know, oddly enough, so do I."

"Oh," I said.

"Maybe it's just a reaction because of Mona and Luisa. But I doubt very much if my God is the same kind of God you believe in, Camilla Dickinson."

"I don't believe in an old man in a nightgown and long white whiskers, if that's what you mean," I said rather sharply.

"Tell me about your God," Frank demanded. "What kind of a God *do* you believe in?"

We walked around the park and I didn't say anything because I was trying to think the kind of God I believe in into words. God wasn't anything I ever thought about at all before I met Luisa. He was just something that was always there, the way Mother and Father were before Jacques. And when Luisa talked to me about God it didn't make me want to think about Him; it just made me stubborn. But Frank made me want to think.

We paused for a moment to watch two old men wearing wool caps and big woolen scarves sitting on a bench with a chessboard between them. They sat as still as statues, almost as though the chill November air had frozen them. We waited until finally one of them reached out a hand in a gray woolen glove and made a move and then Frank walked me over to a bench and pushed me down on it and we sat there and a brown leaf dropped from the tree behind us and drifted down onto the sidewalk.

"Well," I said at last, "I don't think it's God's fault when people do anything wrong. And I don't think He plans it when people are good. But I think He makes it possible for people to be ever so much bigger and better than they are. That is, if they want to be. What I mean is, people have to do it themselves. God isn't going to do it for them." And at the same time that I was saying this and believing it, I was thinking, But why did God let Jacques come?

Frank said, "I like that, Camilla. I like what you said. Sometime I'd really like to have a good talk with you—if Luisa'll let me tear you away."

Again, when he talked about Luisa and me like that, it made me mad, and I said, "That's up to me."

"Well, will you, then, Cam?" Frank asked. "There are so few people in the world anybody can talk to. I mean about things that matter. Most girls your age— well, when you go out with them you know they're always kind of thinking about being kissed. I mean it's all so kind of new to them, that sort of thing, and it makes them kind of one-track-minded. But with you— if anybody notices the way you look in your sweater, it'll be me, not you. And we can talk. Usually a girl you can talk with isn't—doesn't have any—but you do. You sit there and you talk about God and you look just beautiful."

When Frank said that it was as though something warm and lovely had exploded right in the middle of my stomach and, like the sun, sent rays of happiness all through my body. All my misery about Mother and Father and Jacques disappeared from even the darkest corners of my mind, pushed away by the lovely warmth, and I couldn't keep a smile from starting in my eyes and then spreading all over my face the way the warm feeling had spread all over my body.

When I was little I had often heard people say (when they thought I couldn't hear), "What a pity that Camilla looks so like her father instead of Rose." And people were always talking about how beautiful Mother was, but they had never called me a beautiful child. I had thought during the past winter that I must be getting prettier, partly from my own mirror and partly from the way Mother looked at me, pleased, and at the same time wistful and unhappy, as though my changing from the ugly duckling must somehow be taking something from her. But to have Frank say it out loud for me, that I was beautiful, made me dizzy with pleasure.

And then Frank said, "Luisa's ugly as a mud fence, isn't she?"

I stood up furiously and cried, "She is not! She's the most nice-looking person I know!" And I wanted to fly to wherever Luisa was sitting by herself in the movies and put my arms around her and protect her from Frank's words.

"What a little tiger," Frank said. "I didn't mean any harm to your precious Luisa. After all, she's my sister and I'm fond of her even if half the time I'd like to kill her. You should hear the things she says about you sometimes."

"What does she say?"

"Oh—she talks."

"About what?"

"Your mother, for instance."

"What does she say about Mother?"

"Well, I suppose it's true," Frank said. "We seem to love our parents no matter what they're like, even when we hate them."

"But what does Luisa say about Mother?" My voice was fierce.

"I shouldn't have started this," Frank said. "But I don't like people who start things and then back out. She just said once that your mother seems—well, foolish and childish, and that she thinks she must always have been that way, and not just lately. Of course, Cam, you know Lu wouldn't talk about anything like this to anybody but me. We fight a lot but we talk too."

"I guess Mother's always been childish," I said slowly, still thinking over his first words. "What's that got to do with anything?"

"Well, just that Luisa doesn't understand how you used to adore your mother so."

"I've told her," I said to Frank with angry patience. "I've told her again and again. We used to have such fun together. Like two kids. I think it was because Mother *was* childish that we had so much fun. She really liked playing with me, tea parties and make-believe. She was really more fun, she could think of more things to do, than other kids. And we'd tell each other all kinds of things. Now it's different. When we talk to each other it's different. We tell each other different kinds of things. We're not the same people."

"Luisa says she's very pretty."

"That's changed too," I said. "She used to look like a princess in a fairy tale, and now that's gone. I suppose she's still beautiful, but it's different."

"Listen, I'm hungry," Frank said suddenly. "Have you eaten?"

"No." I was grateful to him for changing the subject.

"We could go back to the apartment and dig something out of the icebox, only I'm afraid Mona'll still be there, and Luisa'll come blundering in anytime now, anyhow." He fished in his pockets. "I've got about a dollar. That'll give us each a hamburger and a milkshake. Wish I hadn't wasted a quarter on that putrid movie."

"I can pay for mine," I said.

Frank put the coins back into his pocket and then he took his hands and put them on my shoulders and said, "Listen, Camilla, you know what this is? This is a date. A dinner date. We'll go to Nedick's and pretend it's the Persian Room at the Plaza. Okay?"

"Okay," I said.

We had a lovely time at Nedick's. There was an old woman sitting next to us drinking that awful orange stuff and I think she'd been drinking something else before that because every few sips she would throw back her head and sing, and then she'd give a running commentary on the song and the people in Nedick's; and one of the men kept threatening to throw her out if she didn't keep quiet. Frank and I pretended the old woman was Hildegarde singing in the Persian Room at the Plaza, and the old woman loved it; I think perhaps she'd been an actress once upon a time.

She was so happy because we were laughing and paying attention to her that you couldn't mind about her being drunk, and Frank said, "Sing some Noel Coward for the young lady, Hildegarde," and she shook with laughter and said, "Noel Coward. Now, there was an interesting man, dearie. I met him one day down at the Battery when he was writing the weather reports. You've never heard weather reports like he wrote. Better than singing commercials," and then we all laughed and laughed, and then she started singing "Cockles and Mussels," which seemed to be her favorite song.

We took as long over our hamburgers and hot chocolate as we possibly could, and the old woman had one small orange drink after another; but finally Frank and I had to go, so we left her there, drinking her drink and singing "Cockles and Mussels."

Frank took me to the subway and I thought he was going to take me home, but he said, "I'm sorry I can't ride back with you, Camilla, but I promised David I'd go see him this evening and it's so late already, I'm afraid he'll think I've forgotten him. David's a veteran. He lost both his legs in the war."

"Oh," I said. We stood there at the mouth of the subway for a moment and then I said, "Thank you for the dinner and everything," and Frank took my hand in his and held it, and then I turned and ran down the subway stairs.

All the way home I thought about the way he had told me I was beautiful, and the way he had put his hands on my shoulders and told me we were having a date, and the way he had held my hand when we said good-bye; and for the first time growing up seemed something pleasant to me. Luisa can't wait to grow up and go to medical school and everything, but I've kept having the feeling that if I weren't growing up, everything would be all right with Mother and Father, and Jacques would never have happened.

Once Luisa asked me, "Do you think Jacques is the first one?"

"The first what?"

"Now, Camilla," Luisa said, "don't pretend to be dumber than you are. You know perfectly well what I mean."

So I said, very firmly, "Yes."

And Luisa said, "I hope you're right, Camilla. I sincerely hope you're right," and shook her head in a way that reminded me of Mona. But I knew that I was right. Before Jacques started coming to the apartment everything was all simple and easy; now it is all complicated and difficult.

Before Jacques. After Jacques. I seemed to label everything like that.

But it was a funny thing: while I sat there in the subway on my way home I began to wonder for the first time if Jacques was really the only reason that everything seemed changed, or if he was only, as Luisa would say, the symptom and not the disease. Even before I was really aware of Jacques, things seemed somehow different; sitting there and looking at an ad for corned-beef hash, I had to admit that.

Just the little unimportant things, walking alone down on the beach in Maine on the long summer evenings; tea parties all alone with Mother when we pretended to talk together like two grown-up ladies having tea; sitting very quietly in Father's study while he read his paper and had his cocktail—it was things like these that were beginning to lose their glory before I had even heard of Jacques. And there was the miserable dull aching in my limbs that Mother called growing pains as she gently massaged my legs—but that was also an ache in my heart. Does the heart grow as well as the limbs? Nobody can rub your heart for you to ease the discomfort. That pain had nothing to do with Jacques. It was just easy to blame Jacques, to hate him, for everything.

I wished Frank had not left me at the top of the subway stairs to go see David—though I knew that was selfish and bad of me. Somehow, now, I could not think of the lovely time I had had with Frank but only of the fact that I did not want to be on my way home.

3

The moment I put my key in the latch and opened the door of our apartment I knew that something terrible had happened. All the lamps were on and the place seemed full of a light as sharp and cruel as the light in an operating room. I heard feet running back and forth and then I heard my mother scream and I thought, Father is murdering her, oh God, Father is murdering her; and I went running through the apartment to my mother's room. It was full of people: Father and Dr. Wallace and Carter and the cook, and Mother was flinging herself about on the bed and screaming and Father and Carter were trying to hold her down and there was blood all over the bed.

The cook saw me and cried, "Here's Miss Camilla."

My father said, "Get her out of here."

Dr. Wallace said to the cook, "Get me some boiling water."

The cook pushed out into the hall, taking me with her, and we went into the kitchen and she splashed hot water into the kettle, spilling half of it on the floor, and slopped it onto the stove, turning on the gas, high.

And I thought, Somebody came in time. Somebody came in time to stop Father. And I thought of the newspapers Carter reads, with pictures of women with battered heads on bloody kitchen floors and women lying in satin-quilted beds with bullets through their hearts; and I remembered Carter's eager expression as she reads the headlines—SEX MURDER ON PARK AVENUE or MAN KILLS WIFE AND LOVER IN PENTHOUSE RENDEZOUS, or whatever it might be—and then I saw her face as she tried to hold my mother down, and it looked exactly the same way, only now it was a little frightened too.

"Miss Camilla," the cook said, turning from the stove, and she looked at me with her round face wrinkled up in puzzlement. I thought that all this must be very frightening for poor Mrs. Wilson when she'd only been with us such a short time and didn't know us very well. Now I saw that she did not know what to say to me, and that she was unhappy because I had come home and run into Mother's room when I did; I knew it would make her more unhappy if I asked her what had happened, so I just stood there in the kitchen doorway and stared hard at the knob on the stove that turns on the oven. I stood there until the water began to boil and she lifted it off the stove, and then I moved out of the doorway and stood just inside the dining room.

"Poor lady," Mrs. Wilson said. "Poor Mrs. Dickinson." She went by me with the steaming kettle, saying, "You'd better wait here, Miss Camilla, and I'll come right back to you."

I waited and listened. Now there was hardly any sound from the direction of Mother's room. She had stopped screaming and I wondered quite calmly if she had died. I could be calm about it because it was such an impossible thought that it didn't really seem to have anything to do with me, Camilla Dickinson, personally.

Now the apartment was terribly quiet; then through the quietness came the telephone ringing with frightening shrillness. I ran through the dining room out into the hall to answer it. "Hello," I gasped.

"Hello, Rose?" the voice on the other end of the wire said.

"No."

"Who is this? May I speak to Mrs. Dickinson?" the voice asked, and I knew that it was Jacques's voice.

"No," I said.

"Who is this? Is it Camilla?"

"Yes."

"Camilla, I want to speak to your mother."

"No."

70

"Camilla, is anything wrong? Where's Rose?"

I couldn't think what to say. Jacques's calling just then was as shocking as though he had actually picked up the telephone and struck me with it; and I stood there holding the receiver while the silence seemed to stretch from one end of the wire to the other.

Finally Jacques said, "Camilla, I see that I must talk to you. I'm coming over."

"No," I said then quickly. "You can't come. You mustn't come."

"Then you come and see me," he said. "I'll meet you somewhere. Wherever you say."

"No," I said. "I can't."

"Camilla," Jacques said, "I'm sure you've seen and understood far more than Rose and I realized—about the way we feel about each other. Won't you let me talk to you for a few minutes? For your father's sake as well as Rose's and mine."

"I can't now," I said. "I just can't." I strained my ears wildly for any noise that might come from the silence of my mother's room.

"Tomorrow, then," Jacques said, making his voice very pleading. "Tomorrow when you're through school."

"All right, tomorrow," I said, not hearing myself agreeing, just saying anything so that I could hang up the phone and listen.

"Will you come to my apartment?" Jacques asked. "We can talk more comfortably there than anywhere else. You're still too young for bars, aren't you, little one? I'll expect you at my apartment, then, right after school."

"All right," I said. "All right." And I clamped the telephone receiver back into the cradle.

I heard the door of my mother's room open and shut and Carter in her cold gray uniform came up to me as I stood there by the telephone and said, "Your mother wants to know who was on the telephone, Miss Camilla."

"Luisa," I lied quickly, and sat weakly down. If Mother wanted to know who was on the telephone then she couldn't be dead. Carter turned around and disappeared and I heard the door to Mother's room open and shut, and I just sat there until it opened again and Mrs. Wilson came out and went back to the kitchen and then Carter and Dr. Wallace came out into the hall and Carter held out Dr. Wallace's coat for him and handed him his hat.

Dr. Wallace said, "Good night, Carter. Miss Camilla will let me out," and Carter went back into the kitchen. I knew she would be there, trying to listen, and I hoped that perhaps Mrs. Wilson might talk to her, to keep her from hearing anything.

"Put on your coat and hat, Camilla," Dr. Wallace said. "We'll go out together and have a cup of coffee, and then your mother will want to see you."

I fumbled into my coat, and my hands suddenly seemed so cold and numb that I couldn't get the buttons through the buttonholes; so Dr. Wallace but-

72

toned my coat for me, and took my beret and put it on, saying, "There. That may not be just the fashionable angle, but it looks very nice. I like your red beret and navy blue coat, Camilla," and he smiled at me very kindly. I knew that he was sorry for me and I wanted more than anything in the world to have him not be sorry for me; and I realized what a terrible thing it is to be pitied.

For the first few minutes in the drugstore Dr. Wallace just sat and looked at his coffee and said nothing. We have known him for a long time. When I first remember him he was thin with a lot of thick brown hair. Now he has quite a large stomach and not so much hair.

I sat there and watched him put sugar and cream into his coffee and waited for him to speak; and while I waited I felt almost peaceful because before this moment it had seemed to me that I ought to be able to do something about everything, and now he had taken all responsibility away from me. He seemed serious and when he looked up at me his eyes were probing.

"Camilla," he said at last, "you're going to be a very beautiful woman someday."

This was not at all what I had expected him to say, and I looked so startled that he laughed.

Then he said, "Beauty carries with it a great responsibility, Camilla. A beautiful person should also be a strong person, but many people use their beauty as an excuse for weakness. I've known you since you were small, Camilla, and I think that you can be strong if you want to, and I hope you'll want to."

"I'd like to be strong," I said, though I didn't know what he was driving at.

Perhaps he didn't either, for he said suddenly, "Sometimes when things get too much for people they try to solve their problems by trying to get out of everything altogether. It's not a very good way and fortunately it doesn't always work. Camilla, I think you're old enough and strong enough to face facts. Your mother tried to take her own life tonight."

Sitting there in the steam-heated drugstore, with my navy blue coat still buttoned, I began to shiver. I put my hands on my lap and clenched them to try to stop their shaking, but my body shivered and under the table my legs trembled.

"Let's walk a little," Dr. Wallace said. He put some money on the counter and we left the drugstore and began to walk down Madison Avenue.

"Your mother's really still a child," Dr. Wallace said as he walked. "She's loved and adored you, but you've been more like a wonderful doll than a child to her. You know that marvelous doll that you're giving to your friend Luisa? Your mother would have loved that doll."

"How did you know about the doll?" I asked.

"It's odd, the things a person will talk about when she's hysterical and overwrought. Your mother talked about the doll tonight. Camilla, I wish I could pretend for you that nothing has happened, but I can't. You must just thank God that your father came home when he did, and that I was already on my way to your apartment. Go home to her and love her and be very strong, because she needs strength, and strength, like fear, is contagious."

We turned around then and walked home and Dr. Wallace took me up in the elevator. The elevator boy grinned at me and I wondered if he knew that anything had happened. Dr. Wallace left me at the apartment door and I went in alone. I walked through the apartment until I got to my mother's room. The lamp by the bed was on and she was lying there, asleep. My father sat on a low chair by the bed and his head, dark as an inkstain, was down on the blanket close to Mother, and he was asleep too. Mother looked very white and both her wrists were bandaged in neat white bandages. I stood looking at them for a moment, and then I started to tiptoe out of the room; but, as I turned, my mother opened her eyes and held out her arms to me, and I ran to her and she hugged me and said, "Oh, Camilla, Camilla darling, forgive me," and my father woke up then and the three of us were a tangle of arms and we were full of love and close, close, and I thought, Nothing can ever push us apart again.

I kissed them and I went into my room and undressed and fell into a deep sleep black as velvet and when I woke up it was daylight and I ran into my parents' room and they were lying in bed holding each other close and they smiled at me, and my mother said, "Darling, do you forgive me?"

And my father said, "It was all my fault; it was all my fault," and I left them, each trying louder than the other to take the blame.

On the breakfast table I found two books my father had heard me mention wanting. Carter said, "Your father told me these books were for you, Miss Camilla. I think he brought them home last night. I suppose the poor dear man was too upset to give them to you then."

I looked at Carter but I did not say anything and I ate my breakfast in silence with Carter hovering over me and looking terribly important and knowing; and then I called good-bye to my parents and left for school. And I was happy because I thought that now Jacques was out of the apartment and out of our lives forever and everything would be as it used to be.

Luisa was already in the classroom when I got there and she said in a cold voice, "So."

"So what?" I said, and at her unexpected anger my happiness fled.

"You know what I'm talking about," Luisa told me and pressed her lips together thinly.

"I haven't the faintest idea," I said, and I sat down at my desk and opened the lid and began tidying it. I put all my pencils and pens in my pencil box and arranged my books in neat piles, and Luisa stood by me, scowling ferociously and waiting for me to say I was sorry or ask her what was wrong; and I didn't say anything at all.

Finally she said, "You went out with Frank yesterday evening."

"Yes," I said. "Why not?"

"But you didn't come by the apartment afterward."

"It was late and I had to get home."

"But you're my friend!" Luisa said.

I shut my desk lid firmly. "That doesn't mean I can't be friends with Frank too."

Luisa scowled ferociously. "Frank isn't good for you."

"Oh, shut up," I said.

And then, right there in the classroom, with other girls coming in and out, Luisa burst into tears. It was the first time I had ever seen her cry. I had seen her nearly cry lots of times; but always by stamping, or walking about, or talking in a loud voice, she had been able to stop herself. Now she stood there with her face all screwed up and said, "Oh, golly, somebody'll see me!"

"Stop crying," I said. "Stop crying at once!" I stood up and banged my desk lid for emphasis.

Luisa went over to her desk and lifted up the lid and shut it down on her fingers so hard that the pain in her fingers made her forget everything except the pain and she was able to stop crying. Then she said, "Camilla, what's wrong? I've never seen you like this before." Her voice was small and hurt.

"I'm not any different," I said. I didn't know whether I was telling the truth or a lie.

Luisa took her fingers out from under the edge of the desk lid and held them in her other hand. "I'm sorry if I sounded nasty about Frank." It was the first time she had ever apologized about anything. "But he really isn't good for you, Camilla. He's too old for you anyhow. He's seventeen. I know about people and you don't. He isn't good for anybody. He's let the Mona–Bill business make him awfully neurotic. Sometimes I think boys take things much harder than girls. And he thinks he's such a brain. He thinks he knows everything. And then his moods. He gets into the most gosh-awful glooms. Black as thunder for hours. But I suppose if you want to go on seeing him it's up to you."

"Yes, it is," I said. "But it won't make any difference with you and me."

"No." Luisa sounded sad. "I suppose it won't."

"How're Mona and Bill?" I asked, because I knew she wanted me to ask her.

"Being polite again. Honestly, Camilla, Bill's an awful fool. I think one reason I'm so fond of him is he's such a fool. But I really don't see why he and Mona ever married. He hasn't the slightest idea what Mona's about. Mona's an intellectual and Bill's just an overgrown athlete who thinks he's an intellectual. But actually he's just all brawn and no brain. You know, all biceps and muscles and nothing else. Biceptual."

She looked in her desk and pulled out *Silas Marner*, which we were doing in English, and handed me a piece of paper that was stuck in between the pages. "It's from Frank," she said reluctantly.

I read the note and it said, "This is Friday so you don't have school tomorrow, so you don't have to do homework this afternoon. Let's continue yesterday evening's conversation. My school doesn't let out till after yours so come on down to the apartment with Luisa and I'll pick you up there."

And suddenly as I read the note I remembered my telephone conversation with Jacques that night before. I could not meet Frank because I had to go to Jacques's. I wanted to go to Frank's. I did not want to go to see Jacques, but I knew that I must; and at the thought that I had to see him my heart flipped over inside me like a pancake. I had to see him for Mother, so that I could tell him never to call again, never to come to the apartment again, so that I could tell him that everything was all right with Mother and Father, and Mother didn't care about Jacques anymore.

Before I could stop myself (so strong had the habit of telling Luisa everything become) I blurted out, "I can't see Frank because I have to go see Jacques." And then I wished I had bitten off my tongue. I knew that no matter how many questions Luisa asked me I couldn't ever tell her about Mother, though I knew that if Mona tried to cut her wrists Luisa would tell me.

I wished I hadn't said anything about Jacques. Now Luisa would ask me questions, questions. She might even want to go along with me, and Luisa is the hardest person in the world to put off with any evasion.

Her blue eyes darkened the way they always do when she is excited, and she cried, "You're going to see Jacques!"

"Yes," I said, and just then the bell rang and Miss Sargent came in.

At recess there was a gang of girls around us, and I laughed and talked and acted like a kid just to avoid giving Luisa a chance to get me off into a corner. I even listened while Alma Potter, a girl I don't like, tried to show off and make everybody think how grown-up and sophisticated she was.

"Well," she told us, "I wore my new wine-colored coat this morning and on the bus a cop sat down beside me. He was kind of cute but awful old, of course. And I kept noticing his arm."

"What about his arm?" Luisa asked.

"Well, it kept creeping around me. Well, after all, I'm not going to take that kind of thing from a cop. So I said to him, 'The arm of the law may be long,' I said, 'but it can reach too far.'"

I laughed with the other kids, but all the time I was thinking nastily, I wonder where she heard that?

Anyhow it helped to keep me from having to talk with Luisa. I was afraid that if I did I might blurt out about Mother as I had blurted out about Jacques, and I knew that if I did that I'd hate myself forever. Somehow it's never embarrassed me when Luisa's talked about Mona, but I always find myself wishing she didn't know about Jacques.

But after school I was not able to escape her and she cornered me and said, "I'm going with you."

"I'd rather you didn't." I tried to keep my voice very quiet and firm.

"Oh, I won't go in with you or anything. I just think someone ought to go along with you and wait for you, in case anything goes wrong."

"What could go wrong?" I asked.

"With someone like Jacques, you never know," Luisa said. "Gosh, you're innocent, Camilla. Where does he live?"

Then I realized that I had no idea where Jacques lived. "I don't know," I said blankly. "I said I'd go to his apartment, but I don't know where it is."

"Then we must look it up in the phone book." Luisa sounded brisk and businesslike. "Come on."

In the coatroom there is a phone booth with a phone book, and Luisa dragged me to it and began leafing through the unwieldy pages of the book until she came to the N's. "Nissen, Edward; Nissen, Frances; Nissen, Hans; Nissen, Jacques," she said. Then she looked up at me and grinned. "I wouldn't mind going to see him myself."

Jacques lived on West Fifty-third Street, near the Museum of Modern Art. Somehow I had never imagined him as living in that neighborhood, and I must have passed his house many times when I went to the Museum of Modern Art to study an exhibition for an art class in school or to go to one of the movies with Luisa.

"Well, let's go," Luisa said.

I did not want to go. I wanted to meet Frank.

"We'll take the subway," Luisa said.

"No. We'll walk."

"It'll take much longer," Luisa warned.

"I can't help it," I said. "I'm going to walk."

So we walked. As we walked we passed an apartment building under construction and on the wooden hoarding it said RAFFERTY DICKINSON, ARCHITECT, and my heart swelled with pride, and I said, "This is one of Father's apartments." I wondered whether he was at the office today or whether he was there, right this minute, and whether if we waited I might see him.

But Luisa hurried me on. "We shouldn't have come by here. It would be terrible if we saw your father." When we got to the Museum of Modern Art she asked, "How long are you going to be?"

"I don't know. Not long."

"More than half an hour?"

"Oh, no!" I exclaimed, because I knew that what I had to say to Jacques would not take more than a few minutes.

"Well, I think I'll just go in the museum and look around," Luisa said. "I'll check in the lobby every few minutes and if you're not there in half an hour I'm coming for you. Okay?"

"Okay," I said, and watched her go into the museum.

I wanted to go in with her and look at the picture of the two old ladies picking coal off the railroad tracks and the picture that is called *White on White*, but I walked west until I got to the house where Jacques lived.

This is the house where Jacques lives, I thought. This is the door to the house where Jacques lives. This is the elevator inside the door of the house where Jacques lives. This is the button that says sixth floor in the elevator inside the door of the house where Jacques lives.

I kept on talking to myself like that as though everything were part of a nursery rhyme. I punched the button of the elevator—and I don't like self-service elevators; I'm always afraid they'll get stuck—and the door of the elevator closed as though by an unseen hand and the elevator rose with a whirring noise, slowly, slowly, and somehow it was all like a frightening Grimms' fairy tale. The elevator stopped, the door slid open, and I stepped out and the door closed behind me and there I was, locked into a green-painted hall with five grimly closed doors, each with a brass nameplate over the doorbell. The first nameplate I looked at read JACQUES NISSEN and it was in a high state of polish. I stood there and I could not seem to draw my hands out of my pockets so that I could ring the bell. It was as though my hands had turned into black marble, like the legs of the prince in the fairy tale. I stood there thinking how Luisa thinks I am too old for fairy tales and laughs at me because I still read them; but I also read D. H. Lawrence and J. P. Marquand and Elizabeth Bowen, and I have also read Thomas Mann and the first ten pages of *Ulysses*. And lots of others.

I have also read E. M. Forster and Isak Dinesen, I started to say in a silent and silly argument with Luisa, and then I drew my hand out of my pocket and rang the doorbell. I could hear it ring in the apartment and it didn't sound like a doorbell ring at all, but like the chimes of Big Ben, only somehow turned all silky and effeminate.

Before the bell had finished ringing, Jacques opened the door. I think I had for some reason expected him to be in a dressing gown or something in some way different and glamorous; but he just wore his usual dark suit; and he said hurriedly, "Come in, Camilla, there's a good child. I'm talking on the phone," and he moved quickly through a long dark hall to the living room. His living room was as modern as Mona's, though in a different way. Most of the furniture was black and Chinesey instead of blond and Swedishy; the curtains were black-and-white zebra stripes. Jacques sat on the arm of a flame-colored leather chair and talked on the telephone. He said, "Of course, my darling . . . of course I understand, my beautiful brave girl. . . ." And then he said, "I love you I love you I love you," and made kissing noises into the phone; and I wondered to whom he could be talking. I was angry with him for being able to talk to anybody like that when only so short a time ago he had held my mother in his arms and kissed her the way the young men and women do on the roof of the apartment next to ours.

He hung up and turned to me and smiled and said, "I didn't tell her you'd come to see me. I thought it would be best if we kept this visit a secret just between the two of us." And he stroked the telephone as though it were the person he'd just been talking to.

"You didn't tell who?" I asked.

"Rose. Your mother."

I said in a voice as cold as icicles, "She doesn't want to see you. She doesn't want to see you ever again."

"Did she tell you that?" Jacques asked, smiling.

"No," I said. "But she didn't need to tell me. I know."

Jacques got off the arm of the red chair and went over to a black cabinet from which he took a crystal decanter and two crystal glasses; and a lock of his blond hair fell over his forehead.

"You're not too young for sherry, are you?" he asked me, and without waiting for an answer, he filled one of the glasses with the beautiful amber liquid from the decanter and handed it to me. Then he filled the other glass for himself and put the decanter down on a square black table. "Camilla," he said, "my poor sweet little Camilla," and his soft eyes were suddenly grieving, "you're such a very little girl in spite of your old ways, aren't you? And you hate me very much, don't you? And you want to go on hating me, don't you?"

I didn't say anything. I held my glass of sherry in

my hand and looked at him, and his face seemed very unhappy and very kind, and I had never seen it that way before and it disturbed me.

"I don't want you to hate me, Camilla," he said, "so I'm going to try to explain things to you a little. What I have to explain to you is life itself, and that's the most difficult thing in the world, so you must be patient."

"I can't stay very long," I said.

"Then just listen for as long as you can. And let me tell you a story. A kind of a fairy story. There was once a very beautiful rose living in a garden."

"Mother," I said.

"Yes, it's too obvious an allegory, isn't it? Too pat, too easy. Rose's place in life is to be herself, to be beautiful, to be loved, but not admired. Your father has always wanted to admire Rose, to worship her from a distance, but that is not what Rose needs."

I did not listen. I closed my ears. No matter what Jacques said it would be a lie. Even if he told the truth it would come out of his mouth as a lie. Truth is not just facts.

His voice continued. My mind recorded and then discarded his words.

"And what Rose needs is warmth, and tenderness, and affection. Rose must be emotionally protected. Roses grow only in cultivated gardens, and they must be shielded from the wind and the cold. Whereas your father—your father belongs on the scaffolding of one of his highest buildings, with the wind, rather than a woman's hands, ruffling that black hair of his. Your father is basically a cold man, Camilla, and even his passion I imagine must be as cold as a flame of burning hydrogen erupting from a volcano of ice."

"Father is not cold!" I cried.

"Have you ever seen your father casually put his arms around your mother and hold her?" Jacques asked me.

"Of course," I said. And I tried to remember. And I could not. I thought about what Jacques had said about the flame of hydrogen and it made me think of descriptions I had read of Jupiter, which is so far from the sun that its core is overlaid with thousands and thousands of miles of ice from which flames of hydrogen erupt and spill into seas of frozen ammonia; and I did not know what Jacques meant and I hated him. It was easy to hate him.

Jacques took the decanter and poured a little more into my glass, though I had taken only a sip, and refilled his own. "I've done it all wrong again," he said. "And I brought you a doll. How could I have been so stupid as to bring you a doll! And now I've messed it up all over again. I wanted to make you understand and I've just helped you to keep on hating me. But you don't hate Rose, do you, Camilla?"

"Hate Mother!" I cried. "How could I ever hate Mother!"

"Then do you understand her?" Jacques asked me.

"Children are not supposed to understand their mothers," I said loudly. "Mothers are supposed to understand their children."

This was something I had believed before I met Luisa and that I now knew to be untrue, but I thought that if I said it firmly enough I might be able to believe in it again.

"But you're not a child any longer," Jacques told me.

I said, in an ice-cold voice, as cold as an outer planet, "I am a child. I do not intend to grow up."

"But there are compensations," Jacques said, "I promise you there are compensations."

"I don't want them," I said.

"Listen, Camilla." Jacques came over to me and took my chin in his hand and made me look into his eyes, and again his eyes were as sad as a caged animal's and his eyes made me pity him through my hate. "Listen to me. You think that if you could have stayed a child I might never have come into Rose's life, and therefore into your life. Or that if you had remained a child you might not have understood and therefore you wouldn't have had to be unhappy. But the trouble is that you understand only in part. There is a French saying that to understand everything is to forgive everything."

I moved away from him so that I would not have to keep on looking at his eyes and I said, "It doesn't matter anymore whether or not I understand."

"Of course it matters," Jacques said.

"No. Because Mother isn't ever going to see you again."

"That's not what she gave me to understand when

I talked to her on the telephone just now," Jacques said.

"You didn't talk to Mother!"

"Who did you think it was?"

"I didn't know." But of course I had known, even though I had almost convinced myself because I didn't want to know.

"I called five times," Jacques said. "Four times the maid answered the phone and said that your mother was out and the fifth time she answered herself." His words plunged like brutal stones into the waters of my mind.

I dropped my sherry glass on the floor and I didn't apologize or stop to pick it up but walked out of his apartment and shut his door behind me.

I had thought that I knew what hate was when I hated Jacques, but I only knew it now that I hated my mother.

4

For Jacques my hate had been like the fox inside the Spartan boy's shirt, gnawing away at him, eating him alive. But for my mother it was like a thunderstorm and it was as physical as a thunderstorm. Everything in front of my eyes blackened, as though a huge cloud cut off the light of the sun; but the cloud was inside my head and it was my mind and not the day that was darkened. I walked down the street. I walked past the Museum of Modern Art and never for a moment thought of Luisa. I went into the subway and rode downtown and got off at Eighth Street, though I was thinking neither of Frank nor of Luisa, and when I got out of the subway I did not walk over to Ninth Street but went west to where the streets are crooked.

I walked, turning left or right indiscriminately as

I came to corners, and my body was so full of the black cloud of hate that it was almost impossible for me to breathe, and I had to stop walking and stand very still. I stood in the middle of the sidewalk, looking around me very carefully, not to find out where I was, but to find out who I was, because I was somehow no longer Camilla Dickinson. All that there was in me and around me was a whir of hideous words that buzzed about my head like a mass of hornets, so that the dark cloud seemed no longer like a thundercloud but like a swarm of filthy insects.

A rose is a rose is a rose. That is a quote. But what is a rose? A rose is a rose is a rose tells you nothing. My mother is a rose and what is my mother?

A skinny, mangy-looking dog flashed across the street and a truck skidded over to the curb with a screeching of brakes like the sound of my hate. The dog reached the sidewalk in safety, the truck moved on downtown, and I seemed to wake up as though I had suddenly come out of a nightmare.

It was not that I had stopped hating my mother; but now I could say to myself, I hate my mother. I could put it into words. And I could wonder what I was going to do next. I was no longer driven about the streets like a dead leaf in the autumn wind. Now if I went home or if I went back to the Museum of Modern Art to find Luisa, or if I went to her apartment to find Frank, I would go knowing where I went. But I did not want to go anywhere. I remembered Luisa coming to my apartment and saying she didn't want to go home. I remembered her saying it was silly when I asked her to spend the night because she didn't want to go home, ever. Now I knew how she felt.

I walked slowly down the street and all of a sudden piano music came pouring out of an upper window of one of the houses. It wasn't somebody practicing a music lesson; it wasn't somebody playing carelessly at the piano just for fun, the way Mother sometimes does; it was somebody playing the piano the way a real astronomer would go to a new telescope that might show him an undiscovered star, or the way a scientist on the verge of a tremendous discovery would enter his laboratory; it was somebody playing the piano the way Picasso must have painted his harlequins or Francis Thompson have written "The Hound of Heaven." I stopped and listened and listened. I did not know what the music was, but it made me think of the names of stars, of the winter stars, Aquarius, Capricornus, Pisces, Mesartim, Cetus, Piscium.

I sat down on the rough brown steps leading to the house and leaned my head against the iron railing, because suddenly I was so tired that my legs were ready to collapse under me, and I wanted my mother. I did not want Rose Dickinson who had been talking on the telephone to Jacques Nissen. I wanted my mother. I wanted my mother to come and take me by the hand and lead me home and undress me and put me to bed and rub my head and bring me milk toast and then turn out my light but leave the door open with the light from the hall shining in and then sit by my bed and hold my hand until I fell asleep—the way she did once on a night when I suddenly got a high fever and it was my nurse's night off and Dr. Wallace said I had flu.

But Mother was still in bed with her wrists bound in white bandages and the telephone beside her so that in the end she could not help talking to Jacques.

And I thought, I don't want to be beautiful. I don't want to be like a camellia or a rose or any kind of flower. I wish I had red hair and freckles and a big mouth like Luisa's. I wish people were still saying what a pity it is I don't look like my mother.

Damn beauty, I thought, and wished that God would strike me down for swearing. But that is not the kind of thing the God I believe in does. If there is going to be any striking down you have to do it yourself. God does not do it for you.

The music stopped and suddenly the air about the street seemed empty, as though an element had been taken away from it. What elements is air composed of: oxygen and hydrogen and argon and nitrogen and carbon dioxide? And the cars in the city adding carbon monoxide. And all the smells of the street: beer from the tavern and bananas and onions from the vegetable wagon and the smell of stray dogs and cats. The air on this street had held music, too, and now it left a space that had to be filled up. But the empty place stayed, cold and dark.

What shall I do? I thought. Oh, Mother, where shall I go? But no one answered me and the silence lay against me like a weight.

I sat there. The day left the street, lights came on in the shops and in the windows above the shops, and people walked by in a hurry to get home to dinner. And at last I stumbled to my feet and started walking. I walked without paying any attention to where I was going, but somehow I was not surprised when I turned into Ninth Street. I stopped in front of Luisa's house and I wanted to ring the buzzer and ask for Frank, but I was afraid that Luisa would have given up at the Museum of Modern Art and come back downtown, and I could not, I could not talk to Luisa.

I stood uncertainly in front of the doorway and the door opened and someone came out and started to walk past me and then said in a surprised voice, "Camilla!"

I said, "Frank," and my teeth were chattering inside my head.

"Cam, I'd given you up," Frank said, and then, "What's wrong?"

"Nothing," I tried to say through my chattering teeth.

"Didn't that brat of a Luisa give you my message?" Frank asked. "I wanted you to meet me right after school."

"I couldn't," I said. "I wanted to, but I couldn't. . . ."

Frank was bending over me, a dark shadow trying to peer into my face. "Camilla, you look as though you'd just been knifed. You'd better come upstairs with me. No, Mona and Bill are there. That wouldn't be any good."

"Is Luisa back yet?" I asked.

"Not yet. And we don't want to bump into her. Come on."

"But you were going somewhere. . . ." My voice trailed off.

"Just to the library to get a book. I was mad at you because I thought you'd ditched me." He took my arm and started walking me at such a rapid pace that I almost had to run. "I'm sorry if I'm tiring you," he said once, "but you look so cold I thought we ought to walk fast to try to warm you up." He did not tell me where he was taking me and somehow I was too confused and numb to wonder. All that mattered was that Frank had my arm and that he was taking care of me.

We stopped in front of an old movie theater on a darkish street. I kept numbly beside him while he bought two tickets and took me in. The lobby was dim and hot and stale. A woman with short, straight, gray hair that stuck grotesquely out from her head was swearing at a candy-dispensing machine that would give her neither her candy nor her money back. Frank went over to her and pulled the plungers and in a moment a box of candy dropped into the tray and the woman showered Frank with blessings in a broken accent.

The floor of the lobby had an old worn carpet and was littered with candy papers and cigarette butts and

I stared down at it until Frank led me up two steep flights of stairs and we came out in the top balcony. On the screen a man and a woman were kissing passionately and I thought for a moment that I was going to throw up. Then the woman broke away from the man and screamed at him in Italian and Frank and I climbed to the very back row and sat down. The second balcony was almost deserted; a few people sat in the front rows, but Frank and I were in the back row with empty seats spreading out in front of us and on either side.

"This isn't a bad picture," Frank said. "Mona took me to see it when it was uptown." We sat looking at the screen for a moment, but I couldn't keep my mind on it; the people on the screen seemed to be moving about in complete confusion. I could not clear my head enough to read the English subtitles and find out what the story was about. I put my head down on my knees.

Frank said in a low dispassionate voice, "This used to be a legitimate theater once. Bernhardt played here, and Duse. It's about to fall down and I suppose it'll be condemned soon. But I love to come here."

I tried to look around me, at the faded red velvet of the small boxes, the tarnished gilt of the proscenium, the old gas jets that had been converted into dim red exit lights. Then I looked at the screen again and a woman was lying out in an open field in the rain and weeping; and I began to shiver again.

"Listen, Camilla," Frank said, "you're alive and that's

the most important thing in the world. I mean, nothing too awful can happen as long as you're alive."

I turned around in my seat and looked at Frank, and although I was still shivering I felt quite calm. And I looked at Frank in the darkness with his face flickering from the reflection of the moving light on the screen and it was as though I were looking at him in a dream or as though I were at the bottom of the ocean and looking at him through the weight of millions of tons of water.

"My mother is dead," I said, and my voice came out very calm and as though it were made of glass, like a voice in a dream.

"What!" Frank said.

And then it was as though I had waked up and I was terribly confused and I shook my head and said, "No, no, she isn't dead, she—" and I didn't know what I meant, or what I had meant to say. All the while I had been walking along the streets with Frank, waiting in the lobby while he got the candy from the machine for the gray-haired woman, sitting beside him in the last row of the second balcony, I had been thinking as though Mother were dead, and she wasn't dead. I had been thinking it not because she tried to cut her wrists but because she talked to Jacques on the phone.

"Oh," I said, "oh, Frank, I don't know what to do!"

Sitting there beside me, Frank didn't say anything for a moment, but stared fixedly at the screen. Then he asked, "Do you want to talk about it?"

"I don't know," I said. "I'm just—oh, Frank, I don't know what to do."

"Listen, Camilla," Frank said, and then he said to me what he had already said, "listen, Camilla, you're alive. As long as you're alive that's the most important thing in the world. People die, young people, who haven't ever had any chance, and it's awful, and they're the ones you cry about because they're dead and they haven't got any more life again, ever. But you're alive and as long as you're alive everything's really all right, in spite of everything else. No matter what happens, as long as you're alive everything's all right."

But all of a sudden I didn't want to be alive. I thought that if I were dead I would not know about Mother talking to Jacques or trying to cut her wrists or kissing Jacques in the living room (and where else had she kissed him, how many other times?), and I wouldn't be feeling as though I were in a nightmare and I wouldn't be wondering what I was going to do. "I don't think I want to be alive," I said. "I think I'd rather be dead."

Then Frank grabbed me by the shoulders and started to shake me, and shook me and shook me until my teeth chattered in my head and I started to cry. Then he released me and flung himself back in his seat.

"I'm sorry." His voice was shaky with rage. "But you made me do it. You made me."

We sat silent for a long time then, with Frank glowering at the screen, and by and by I began to watch, too, sitting there with my hands clenched in my lap and my tears still distorting my view of the people in the picture. After a while Frank's hand came down firmly over mine. He didn't say anything, but I knew that it was all right between us again.

Then all of a sudden I remembered Luisa, Luisa whom I had left waiting in the Museum of Modern Art, and I felt the blood rushing to my face in horror at the awful thing I had done to her.

"Luisa," I whispered to Frank. "Luisa!"

"What about her?"

"I left her in the Museum of Modern Art. I promised her I'd go back for her and I forgot. I forgot all about her."

"Don't worry about Luisa," Frank said. "She'll be home by now."

"But—but—" I stammered. "I was—someplace—and she said if I didn't come back in half an hour she would go for me there—and it would be awful if she did—and if she got worried and called home it would be terrible."

Frank sighed. "I suppose we'd better call her. Come on." He stood up and I followed him down the stairs. A girl with a great mop of dark curly hair was standing in the lobby waiting, while a boy in a red turtleneck sweater got candy out of the machine. She grinned at Frank and stared at me and said, "Hi, Franky, honey."

"Hi, Pompilia," he said, nodded at the boy in the red sweater, and hurried me out of the theater.

The air outside was clean and wonderful and we stood breathing it for a moment. Then we walked to a cigar store where there was a telephone booth. I dropped in my nickel and dialed, and almost immediately Luisa answered, saying "Hello" in a loud voice, because she had either the phonograph or WQXR on very high and I could hear the music blaring into the telephone.

"Oh, Luisa," I cried in relief. "Oh, Luisa!"

"Wait'll I turn the radio down," Luisa shouted, and in a minute the sound of music almost disappeared and Luisa was back at the telephone. To my relief she didn't sound angry, just excited. "Camilla, wherever are you!" she exclaimed. "Your mother and father are having fits!"

"You didn't tell them about my going to see Jacques!" I cried.

"What kind of a dope do you think I am? Of course I didn't. Where are you? Whatever happened to you? I waited and waited and then I went to Jacques's apartment and rang the bell. I pretended I was looking for someone I thought lived there, but I got a good enough look around to see that you weren't there. So don't worry, Camilla, I haven't compromised you any with Jacques. He didn't have the slightest idea who I was or that I was looking for you."

"But what about Mother and Father?" I said. "You didn't tell them. Luisa!"

"Listen, what do you think I am, a stool pigeon?"

Luisa asked. "They've been phoning here ever since I got home. Mona and Bill went out after I came in and God knows where Frank's off to, so I've had the place to myself, and I gave them no information whatsoever. But you'd better call them up and tell them you're alive because your mother was weeping like mad."

"All right," I said. "I'll call her. Thanks, Luisa, for not telling and everything."

"That's okay, but what happened and where are you now?" Luisa demanded.

"I'll tell you later," I said. "Good-bye. I'd better call home right away."

"Well, when am I going to see you?" Luisa asked.

"Tomorrow at school."

"Tomorrow's Saturday."

"Well, tomorrow sometime. Let's go to a movie." If we went to a movie we wouldn't have to talk so much.

But Luisa said, "I haven't even a quarter for a Forty-second Street one."

"I'll take you."

"No," Luisa said. "I want to talk to you. You can't get out of it that way, Camilla. Come on down to the apartment in the morning and we'll take Oscar for a walk. He needs exercise."

"All right," I said. "Maybe."

"Camilla," Luisa said at the other end of the wire, "it isn't good for you to try to keep things inside yourself the way you do. That's the way you get inhibitions. I've had to absolutely guess everything about your mother and Jacques. You haven't told me anything yourself."

"Well, if you guessed," I said, "I didn't need to."

"But I can't guess what happened this afternoon and if you keep it inside you'll get all kinds of traumas and things. I'm absolutely sure it was a traumatic experience, and if you tell me all about it, it'll keep it from leaving scars. I wish you'd let me psychoanalyze you. I know it would help."

"No," I said.

"Well, what time are you coming down?"

"I don't know. Sometime."

"Camilla, I thought we were best friends."

"We are."

"Then come on down tomorrow morning first thing."

"Okay," I promised, because there was no way out of it.

"Till tomorrow, then."

"Okay, good-bye," and I hung up. I opened the door of the phone booth and told Frank, "I have to call my mother now."

He nodded, then asked me, "Did you tell Luisa you were with me?"

"No. I didn't tell her where I was."

"Good girl," Frank said.

I shut the door of the phone booth again and dialed home. My father answered the phone and I said, "Father, this is Camilla."

102

Right away he called out, "Rose, it's Camilla!" and then he said to me, "Camilla, we've been worried about you. Where have you been?"

And then my mother's voice came into the phone and I could imagine her snatching it out of my father's hand. "Oh, Camilla, darling, darling, I've been frantic! Where have you—what's happened to you?"

I couldn't say I'd been with Luisa because they'd been calling Luisa, so I just said, "Nothing's happened to me. I'm perfectly all right," in a cold voice, and felt no pity for my mother still sounding frantic on the other end of the wire.

"Where are you—come home, come home at once!" my mother cried.

"I'll be home by my bedtime," I said.

"Camilla, what is it? Why are you talking this way? Where are you? Come home, come home," my mother cried, and I wanted to put my hands over my ears or simply hang up to end the conversation, but I could not put the phone down on that wild voice going on and on. . . .

Then my father's voice came again. "Camilla, I don't know what all this nonsense is about, but you are to come home at once."

When I heard his voice, so angry and so unhappy, I felt whipped, and I said, "All right. I'll come." I hung up and left the phone booth. "I've got to go home," I said.

Frank dug his gloves out of his pocket and put them on. "I'll take you. Come on."

"Thank you," I said, and my voice felt like a lead weight being dropped.

As we got to the house Frank said, "I'll meet you on the steps of the Metropolitan Museum at nine o'clock tomorrow morning."

"I can't. I promised Luisa I'd—"

"Oh, blast Luisa," he said. "Okay, then I'll rescue you from her clutches right after lunch."

"Thank you," I said, and I thought, If only I could stay with Frank now. If only I didn't have to leave him.

When I got home it was as though I were a can and Mother and Father were can openers, trying to pry me open. Why had I just gone off after school that afternoon? Why hadn't I come home for dinner? Why hadn't I telephoned them right away? If I abused the privileges they gave me then my freedom would have to be taken away. What had I been thinking of?

And I just kept staring down at my feet in my brown school shoes and saying, "I don't know."

And when my mother, sitting up in bed with her bandaged wrists and weeping, asked me, "Oh, my darling, don't you love us anymore?" all I could answer was, "I don't know."

Then my father took me into his room and sat down in his red leather chair at his desk; I stood by his side as though I were a wayward student and he the teacher, and he said, very gravely, "Camilla, I don't understand your behavior."

I said, "I'm sorry."

Then he said, as though it were very difficult for him, "I blame myself for it. I shouldn't have asked you the questions I did when I took you out to dinner the other night. I was—I was not myself."

"No," I said. "It wasn't that."

"Then what?" he asked me.

"I don't know," I said.

Then he tried to explain it to me in his way, just as Jacques in the afternoon had tried to explain it in his: "Camilla, your mother is a very beautiful woman."

"Yes," I said.

"And Nissen is a very clever man. He flattered your mother, and perhaps he turned her head for a brief time. However, it wasn't important, and the blame is Nissen's, and not your mother's. It's all over now, between your mother and Nissen, anyhow. Whatever little there was is finished." I looked at him and I wondered if he thought he was telling the truth or if he was just saying what he thought I wanted or ought to hear; but his face was set in the immovable lines of the statues of the Roman senators in the Metropolitan Museum and his eyes seemed almost as blind and blank as those of the statues.

But truth seemed to be changing. I had thought that truth was always simple and clear. A thing was true or it was a lie. But now, as time seemed simultaneously to stand still and to rush by me with the startling speed of a meteor, I knew that truth was as complicated as time.

Then, "Camilla," my father said, "I know that you're

at an age when things have a profound effect on you. But you must remember that the things you do also have their effect on other people. After what—what happened to your mother last night, it was not kind of you, to say the least, to run off this afternoon. I want you to go in to her now, and tell her that you love her and that you're sorry."

I asked my father then a strange question, one that popped out of my mouth without my expecting it to, and that surprised me as much as it surprised my father.

"Father, was I an accident?"

My father sat very still for a moment; then he said, "What do you mean?"

"Did you and Mother want to have a child?" I asked. "Or did I just happen?"

"Of course we wanted a child," my father said. "I wanted a child terribly." But he did not look at me. He looked down at the blotter on his desk and made a group of strange markings on it with his pencil. He said, "I think you're seeing too much of Luisa Rowan. You've had all kinds of strange ideas since you've known her. Why don't you see more of the other girls at school?"

"I do," I said. I wished I hadn't asked the question because now I knew the answer.

My father looked at me and he said, "Camilla, you mustn't be so unhappy. Everything's going to be all right."

He put his hand on my shoulder and I wanted to

hold him and tell him how very terribly much I loved him so that he would never know that the fifth time my mother had answered the telephone herself, but I just stood there under the strength of his hand until he said, "Go in to your mother."

I went to my mother's room. She said, "Oh, Camilla, how could you, how could you?"

I said, "I'm sorry."

And my mother said, "Tell me you love me."

"Mother," I said, "are you ever going to see Jacques again?"

"Oh, of course not, of course not," she said, moving her head back and forth on the pillow. She looked white and delicate and there were tears in her beautiful eyes. "Oh, Camilla, Camilla darling," she said, "there was never anything to it, never anything to have made all this terrible mess. I was just—oh, my baby, tell me you love me."

And I thought, How can I tell her I love her when I don't love her? When I look down at her little white face on the pillow and all I feel is cold, cold, as though there were an icy wind blowing into my heart? I did not even feel hate any longer, but just a cold numbness, as though I'd been given a shot of Novocain that chilled my entire body. I turned and walked out of the room. I felt that I was doing a terrible thing but I could not, I could not do anything else. I went to my room and I got undressed and I was tired. I was so tired that it was too much effort to take a bath or even to brush my teeth or wash my hands and face.

I pulled on my pajamas and got into bed and lay there with the door into the hall closed tight. I tried to say my prayers. I said "Our Father," but it didn't mean anything.

I was almost asleep when the door opened and my mother came in. I opened my eyes and stared at her through the darkness of the room and the fog of my sleep, while she leaned against the post of my bed as though she could hardly stand up.

"I couldn't let you go to sleep without kissing you good night," she whispered, and she bent down and kissed me. When she left me, the fragrance of her perfume stayed behind her. It was perfume she had worn for Jacques and somehow she was still dead.

5

I got up and had breakfast with my father the next morning, but I could not talk to him and he could not talk to me, though once he said, "Camilla, somehow I should have been able to keep this from touching you." Then, when he was finishing his second cup of coffee, he said, "Somehow it's been all my fault. I've done everything wrong. You mustn't blame your mother." Then he said, "Well, I'm going to the office."

I said, "Yesterday I passed an apartment house of yours, Father. Is it going well? Is it going to be a beautiful apartment house?"

My father shook his head. "No, it's not. There was to be sunlight in every room, and space to breathe, and a feeling of the beauty of the city as you looked out the window; but my plans have been taken and distorted and cramped, and now it is just going to be expensive. Very very expensive."

"Are you working on anything that is beautiful now?" I asked him.

"Yes," my father said. "I am designing a small private museum that is very beautiful, and it is that that is keeping me alive." Then he smiled at me and said, "My funny little old woman. Keep your head in the stars, my darling; you see how you can be hurt when you get involved in the things that are happening on earth."

I wanted to tell him that an astronomer, to be a good astronomer, has to have his feet planted very firmly on the earth, otherwise what would his discoveries mean? What could he do with them? But my father got up from the table and came around to me and kissed me on the top of my head quickly, which is the way he always kisses me, and in a moment I heard the front door slam behind him.

I went down to Luisa's. Mona let me in. Oscar jumped up and down and tried to lick my face, then took up his usual place as close to Mona as possible. Even though I have never seen her do anything but scream at him, the dog worships the ground that Mona walks on, and this fact always makes me feel that Mona has more niceness in her than I have ever noticed.

It's a funny thing about Mona. She's a good-looking woman; she certainly dresses well and when I've seen her occasionally with other grown-ups she's been witty and vivacious. Yet when I think of her I always see her in my mind's eye as a woman with a scarred face. I wonder if it's because her spiritual scars somehow speak from somewhere deep inside her to somewhere deep inside me, and somehow get visualized as though they were scars of the flesh. That sounds like Luisa, but it's the only way I can express it.

Now Mona said to me abruptly, "Sit down and talk to me. I sent Luisa out to buy some coffee. Saturday morning and no coffee in the house. Come on. Sit down."

I sat down on a chartreuse-covered chair and Mona sat on a very low sofa and put her feet up on the cluttered glass top of the coffee table. She reached for a half-empty glass and took a swallow and I realized that she was drunk. Not very drunk, but drunk enough to ask me to sit down and talk, something she would never have done ordinarily. Luisa had told me that sometimes on weekends her mother drank too much; I had never seen it before; I had never seen anybody I knew drink too much, and it startled me.

"Well, and how are you this morning, little Miss Iceberg?" Mona asked me. "Happy as a nasty, cold-eyed sea gull?"

I didn't say anything. I looked down at my feet and wished that Luisa would hurry back with the coffee or that Frank or Bill would appear, but it seemed that Mona and Oscar Wilde and I were alone in the apartment.

Mona poured herself another drink. "You know

what Luisa, my own daughter, told me this morning?" she demanded. "You know, hah?"

"No," I said.

"She told me she would like to die. What a thing for a child to say to her mother! Would you like to die, Camilla?"

"No," I said, and it was true. I no longer had my desire of the night before for oblivion, and I was filled with an ache of pity for Luisa, whom I had treated so shabbily.

"No?" Mona asked. "Why not, hah? Sometimes I wonder why people value life so highly, why I haven't killed myself, put an end to the wallowing in misery like a pig in the mud. It isn't my unselfish love for my children. Frank and Luisa can both get along very well without me. Probably better than with me. What a way to bring kids up, anyhow, in the middle of a filthy city. Kids shouldn't be brought up in the city. Kids who're brought up in the city aren't kids. They're —they're like Frank and Luisa, they know too much. Or they're cold little clams like you."

"I'm not cold," I said.

"Hah," Mona said. "I was brought up with elm trees and a big backyard. That's what I should have given Frank and Luisa. Middle West solidity. Everything I had to escape from."

The door banged open then and Luisa hurried in with a bag of marketing. "Hi, Camilla, sorry if I kept you waiting," she said in a falsely casual voice. "I won't be a moment." Then she turned to Mona. "I'll make you a pot of coffee in a minute, Mona. Meanwhile you might leave Camilla alone."

She went into the closet-kitchenette and I heard her turn the water on full force and bang the coffeepot down on the stove.

Mona started to laugh, and laughed and laughed, her head flung back against the sofa, the tears of this strange mirth streaming down her cheeks. "You see," she gasped. "What did I tell you!" Then she finished her drink, put her glass very carefully down on the table, and said in a voice that was suddenly low and sober, "Why is the fear of death so much greater than the fear of life? I'm so ghastly afraid. If I weren't so afraid, I'd have been dead long ago. Maybe it's because we realize—oh, subconsciously, subconsciously of course—that life is a tremendous gift, and we're afraid of losing that gift because—oh, hell, I don't want to be blotto. Even if I'm in agony I'm alive. Oh, how much easier a time people had of it when they had religion."

She stopped short and said, "Luisa told me to leave you alone. I'm not leaving you alone. Why did Luisa tell me to leave you alone? Because I might tell you that some people in this world actually live, actually feel? What would you know about it? You're one of the protected ones. No worries. Parents who wrap you up in cotton wool and guard you from life. You'll wake up someday and then you'll be hurt. It'll do you good to be hurt. Why should my kids be the only ones to be hurt?"

Luisa came in with the coffeepot in one hand and

a cup and saucer in the other. She put the cup and saucer down on the glass coffee table, filled the cup, then banged the coffeepot pot down beside it; there was a sound like the report of a shot, and the glass top of the coffee table cracked right across.

"Damn it!" Mona screamed. "Why can't you be more careful! Get out of here and leave me alone! Both of you! Get out!"

Luisa grabbed me by the hand and we hurried into her room. She sat down on the bottom bunk of her double-decker bed. "Mona's drunk," she said flatly.

"Yes." I wanted to say something else but there was nothing else to say. I couldn't say she wasn't drunk, because she was; and I couldn't say it didn't matter, because it did.

"I don't know why she drinks," Luisa said. "If she got happy when she drinks the way Bill does I'd understand it better. But she just gets like this. It never gives her a lift. And then she feels lousy on Monday when she has to go back to work. I will say for her she never drinks on a weekday. I'm sorry you had to see it, Camilla. I think if you were anybody else and you saw her this way I'd have to kill you."

"I know," I said, because I knew.

"I don't know what she said to you," Luisa went on, "but she didn't mean it. She always says awful things to people when she's drunk. If she talked to you at all it means she really likes you. She just won't speak to people at all when she's drunk if she doesn't like them. But I'm sorry."

"That's okay," I said clumsily. Then I said, "Luisa, if you still want to psychoanalyze me, it's okay."

As I said this Luisa's face lit up and I knew that the gift I had offered her was the right one.

"Honestly?" she exclaimed.

"Honestly."

"But I've been trying to get you to let me for ages and you never would— Well, come on, let's get going! What am I waiting for!"

"I don't know," I said. "Go ahead and start." I was not looking forward to being psychoanalyzed and I wanted to get it over with as soon as possible. I don't think all this probing business is good for people. It's just a good excuse to talk about yourself and I don't much like to talk about myself.

She got up and went to her desk and found a pad and pencil. "Well . . ." she said, and began tapping the pencil against her teeth and thinking.

I sat down and waited and looked about the room while I waited so that I would not start thinking about myself or problems.

I like Luisa's room. It's painted yellow, and around the wall of the bottom bunk of her double-decker she has pasted a frieze of postcards she's bought at various museums. Under the frieze sit her dolls. They use the bottom bunk and she sleeps in the top bunk.

But now she said, "Please get up, Camilla," and swept up all the dolls and said, "I have come to a great decision."

"What?" I asked.

"Well, I thought you should lie down here as though it were a psychiatrist's couch, and then I wondered what to do with the dolls. And then I decided. I am sixteen. I am a woman. If I still like dolls it must be neurotic. So I am going to send them all over to the hospital. Even the one from Jacques that you gave me. You don't mind, do you?"

"No," I said, "of course not." I'd be just as happy not to have to see that doll.

Now she dumped them all into the corner. "Okay, let's begin," she said in a businesslike way, but I could tell she was excited and pleased at the prospect. "Would you mind if we pretend I'm a real psychiatrist? And you're a real patient? I mean, would you mind if we pretend we don't know each other?"

"Okay," I told her. "Anything you say."

She sat down at her desk then. "What is your name, please?"

"Camilla Dickinson."

"And your age?"

"Fifteen."

"Place of birth?"

"Manhattan."

"Now, would you mind lying down there on the couch, please?" Luisa said, pointing to the lower bunk.

I lay down and stared at the slats and the springs of the upper bunk, and through them at the blue of the mattress ticking, and, at the sides and foot of the bunk, the tucked-in edges of sheets and blankets.

"Now, Miss Dickinson," Luisa said eagerly, "please

tell me exactly what happened between you and Jacques Nissen yesterday afternoon."

But this I could not, could not do. Even though I had seen Mona drunk I could not tell Luisa that Mother had talked to Jacques again after everything. I had offered to be psychoanalyzed because that was the only thing I had to offer her because of having seen Mona drunk, but I could not in turn show her my own mother naked as I had seen Mona. In any case I did not think her question was fair; I thought she was taking advantage of the psychoanalysis, so I said, "If you're the psychiatrist and I'm the patient and you've never met me before, then you don't know about Jacques Nissen."

Luisa's eyes darkened with irritation. "Okay, then. What man has had the most influence on your life in the past few months?"

This wasn't fair either. "I don't think a psychiatrist would begin an interview like that." I looked at one of Luisa's postcards, a Marie Laurencin lady who reminded me of Mother, and kept my eyes averted from Luisa. "But if you must know his name it's Frank Rowan." I knew that I was making Luisa angry and the awful part was that now I was doing it deliberately. It wasn't really that I wanted to anger Luisa, because I had honestly and truly offered to be psychoanalyzed just to please her; it was as though I had a little imp sitting in my ear whispering malicious things for me to say.

"Frank isn't a grown man," Luisa said.

"The other day you said he was," I reminded her. "You said he was too old for me and you're always saying I'm a grown woman."

"Okay," Luisa said. "Let him be important to you if you want to get hurt. I've never seen Frank stay interested in any one girl for more than a couple of months. Pompilia Riccioli lasted almost three months. That's about the longest."

I knew, I knew she was saying this just to upset me because she did not want me to like Frank. And she succeeded; I was upset. I remembered the pretty girl Frank had spoken to in the movie lobby the night before. So I just said, staring at another in the frieze of postcards, an angel of Lauren Ford's, "If you're going to analyze me you'd better get on with it."

"You have to cooperate," Luisa said. "The analyst can't do anything unless the patient cooperates."

"I'm cooperating."

"You aren't," Luisa said. "You're bucking me at every step. And you've got to be completely truthful."

"I am being truthful. But I thought analysts began at the beginning. You're beginning at the wrong end. You're supposed to go back practically to—to pre-natal influences," I finished impressively.

Luisa sighed. "Okay, I'll begin at the beginning. But stop looking at the postcards. They're taking your mind off the subject. Now think hard. What is your very first memory?"

My very first memory? I had never thought about it before and I tried to turn my mind back, back, to make up to Luisa for having spoiled the beginning of her analysis. The first thing I could remember was lying in a crib at night and waiting for my mother to come in and say good night to me—no one specific night but just a vague general blur of warmth and security and lamplight and my mother wearing an evening dress and smelling wonderful, wonderful, as she leaned over and kissed me and called me little loving names. And then she would go out and part of the wonderful fragrance would remain behind.

And then I remembered sometimes going into her room in the evening before Binny put me to bed. She would be sitting at her dressing table, and her evening dress, freshly pressed and still smelling faintly of the hot iron, would be laid out across her bed. And she would have her beautiful hair tied back with a dark blue velvet ribbon and she would be smoothing the tiniest bit of rouge into her cheeks and on her lips and touching perfume behind her ears and to the delicate blue veins on her wrists. Then she would take the velvet ribbon off and let me brush her hair, and I remembered that I felt terribly important, standing behind her at the dressing table, passing the silver-backed brush gently over her hair.

These were the first things I remembered, and I told Luisa.

She was sitting at her desk busily jotting things down. "Very interesting, very interesting indeed," she said. "Both of those memories deal with your mother. What is your first memory of your father?"

I tried to think. "I can't decide what is my very first memory of Father," I said at last. "When I was little he always seemed sort of somehow like God. Oh, I do remember one lovely thing."

"What?"

"It's a Christmas memory," I said. "I'm not sure which Christmas, but it must have been an early one because I was terribly excited about going out after dark."

"That's nothing," Luisa said. "You still are. I've never known anybody as protected as you, Camilla."

"Half the kids at school, at least."

"I didn't mean to interrupt," Luisa said quickly. "Go on about your father."

"Well—I remember Binny dressing me up in my best coat and leggings, and—"

"Who's Binny?"

"She was my nurse. And Mother and Father and I went downstairs and got into a taxi and drove all around New York looking at the Christmas trees."

"Very expensive," Luisa said.

"It was beautiful. I sat on Father's lap and he kept his arm around me, so that I felt completely safe shut out in the dark of the night, and we saw the trees up and down Park Avenue and the big tree at Washington Square and the big tree at Radio City and all the trees the driver could find. We even went to Brooklyn and The Bronx."

Luisa nodded and wrote some more things down in her notebook. She wrote very rapidly and I wondered if she would be able to read it afterward. Even when she writes carefully her writing looks like henscratching; half the time she can't decipher her assignment book and has to call me up to find out what the homework is.

Then she looked up and shot at me, "Camilla, what do you know about sex?"

"I—I don't know," I said. "I know about it, I guess."

"Well, didn't your mother tell you or anything?"

"Of course!" When I was ten Mother gave me a very pretty book about flowers and animals and babies, illustrated with beautiful photographs of apple blossoms and a litter of tiny clean pigs and a funny ancient-looking baby holding its knees up to its chest. "You'd better get on with psychoanalyzing me," I said. "That doesn't have anything to do with anything."

"Your reactions do," Luisa told me seriously. "But if you want to do the talking it's okay with me."

"It's not that I want to talk—"

"Oh, forget it." Luisa wrote something else in her notebook and then said in her most impressive, the-famous-Dr.-Rowan way, "You know, don't you, that you, Camilla Dickinson, are completely different from anybody else in the world, that no two human beings are ever alike?"

"Well, of course!"

"Now, can you tell me when you first became aware of yourself as an individual?"

"I don't know," I said. Then, "Yes, I think I can."

Luisa smiled with satisfaction. "One very good thing

about you and me, Camilla, we both have excellent memories. I suppose it's necessary for our professions. Go on. Go on."

"Well," I started, "it's kind of complicated. It's a whole lot of things combined. I mean, that's why it's something I really remember so I couldn't ever forget it even if I wanted to. I don't think it's an awfully easy thing to discover you're yourself and nobody else can be you and you can't be anybody else. It's sort of lonely."

"How old were you?" Luisa asked.

"I don't remember. It started the night before my birthday, but I don't remember which birthday. I couldn't sleep because I was so excited. You know, the way you get the night before your birthday or Christmas. The next day was going to be Sunday so Mother and Father would be with me all day long and I might be able to go skating with Father on the pond in the park and there would be presents and I could stay up half an hour later."

I looked up at the slats and I wasn't seeing them because I was looking back into the past; it was as though I were talking to myself and not to Luisa; and my voice sounded a little sleepy, almost as though Luisa were hypnotizing me. I'm sure she was trying to, the way she sat there leaning forward in her chair, staring at me with such intensity in her blue eyes that I had to turn my own eyes away from her and back to the slats of the upper bunk each time I turned my head to speak to her directly.

"Don't leave out any details," she said. "Tell me everything. Sometimes it's the littlest things that are the most important."

"Well . . ." I said, "I lay in bed staring up at the pattern of light on the ceiling from the rooms across the court, from the rooms of the people who hadn't gone to bed yet—the way I do now. And then I slipped out of bed, because I was so excited, and stood by the window and looked across the court. In one of the windows was the shadow of someone undressing behind a drawn shade, someone pulling a dress over her head, and then a slip, and bending down to take off shoes and stockings. And then all of a sudden I wondered: What was she thinking while she got undressed? What *did* other people think? What did other children think when they weren't with me? Then it suddenly struck me that I hadn't ever realized that they thought at all when they weren't with me. I turned away from the window, and I was frightened, because people must think when they get undressed at night, not only people across the court, but strange people on the street, people I passed walking to the park, and children in the park. It still frightens me."

"Yes," Luisa said, as I paused. "Oh, yes, Camilla, I know what you mean. It frightens me too. Go on."

"Well," I said, "I remember that I turned on the light and stood in front of the mirror, looking at myself, frightened because people thought when they were getting ready for bed and didn't think about me because I wasn't the most important thing in their lives at all. Mother and Father'd always made me feel that I *was* important, and now all of a sudden I realized I wasn't. How can you be important if nobody knows about you? It's very frightening to realize all of a sudden that you aren't important after all. So I stared hard at my face in the mirror, sort of for comfort, because here I was, and I was Camilla Dickinson, and this was my world, only all of a sudden it was everybody else's world too. I started to cry. I got back in bed and cried and cried and called for Mother and she didn't come. Nobody came. Somebody had always come when I cried."

"Frank used to come when I cried," Luisa said. "When I had a bad dream or something. Of course I didn't cry often. But Frank used to be awfully nice to me when I was a kid. He's certainly changed. Go on."

"Well," I said, "finally my father came in to me; he was very gentle and kissed me. It's funny, but whenever Father *did* take care of me, I felt much safer with him than I did with Mother. And he gave me a drink of water and told me 'The Three Bears' (that was my favorite story) and told me to go right back to sleep. So I guess I must have. The next morning I woke up early—you know, the way you always do on your birthday or Christmas, and I still felt kind of funny.

"I went back to the mirror. The floor felt cold on my bare feet. I stood there looking at this other person in the mirror who looked just like me, and all of a sudden I wasn't thinking at all. This other person in the mirror was someone and I was someone and I wasn't sure who because I didn't know either of us and we weren't the same person and I wasn't there at all, because I wasn't thinking, because my mind was quite blank. And then something seemed to go click. This is me. I am Camilla Dickinson. I'm me, and this is what I look like standing on the floor with my feet just off the edge of the rug, staring into the mirror in my room. This is my birthday, this is the birthday of Camilla Dickinson, and I'm a real person just like the people across the court, like the one who got undressed with the shades down, like people on my way to the park. I am Camilla Dickinson and no one else and no one else is me. And then I didn't mind so terribly because people didn't think about me. And then I was frightened again and wanted to cry only I knew that I mustn't because I still believed that if you cried on your birthday you cried every day for the rest of the year."

"I remembered when I discovered I was myself too," Luisa said, "but it wasn't like that. It was once when I got mad at Frank in the park and threw a stone at him and it hit him on the head and knocked him out and I thought I'd killed him and all of a sudden I realized I was the one who'd done it. It's fascinating, isn't it, Camilla? I wonder if everybody remembers. Do you think they do?"

"I don't know," I said.

Then Luisa picked up her pad and pencil again and

wrote something and said, "Well, why didn't your mother come in to you? Was she sick or something?"

"Yes. She was awfully sick. I think she nearly died."

"Did they take her to a hospital?" Luisa asked, with quick interest in any details of illness or hospitals.

"Yes. The morning of my birthday. It was the most awful birthday I ever had."

"Did you go to the hospital to see her?"

"Yes. My grandmother came, Grandmother Wilding, and took me in a taxi. And I remember what a peculiar ride it was."

"Why?"

"Well—everything seemed so much worse because the people we passed on the street didn't know about Mother's being sick or about its being my birthday or how frightened I was. They just went on the way they always do, as though nothing had happened."

"Yes," Luisa said, "I know. It's funny how it helps just if people know things, isn't it? I mean, after Mona and Bill have had a fight I don't seem to mind so much after I've told you about it and I know you know about it too. They didn't tell you what was the matter with your mother?"

"No. I guess I was too young to wonder. I was just frightened. I thought if Mother had to be in the hospital on my birthday she was going to die."

"Well, go on," Luisa said.

"We went to the hospital. I hadn't ever been in a hospital before, and I'm still sort of terrified the way I was that day."

126

"I love hospitals," Luisa said. "When I'm a doctor I want to live right in the hospital. Go on."

"Well, that's all, really. Mother was in the hospital for a couple of weeks and then she came home and—well, that's all."

Luisa wrote busily for a moment, and then she said, "That's very interesting, very interesting," and then she gave a funny sort of shamefaced grin and said, "Golly, Camilla, I guess I must have an awful lot to learn if I want to be a psychiatrist. I ought to have been able to find out an awful lot from what you've just told me. I mean I ought to know about why you have complexes and things and what makes you act the way you do now, and the way you still keep talking about grown-ups as though you were still a child and everything, and I really don't know if I've found out anything at all. Well, one thing I'm learning from psychoanalyzing you is how much I don't know. You really don't know what was the matter with your mother?"

"No. I don't remember whether they told me or not."

"I wonder if she was having a miscarriage."

"I don't know." I felt disturbed, because that had never occurred to me. I don't know a great deal about things like that and they don't seem to enter my head as they do Luisa's.

"When did you first want to become an astronomer?"

Again I shook my head. "I don't really remember.

Always, ever since I can remember. My grandmother used to tell me the names of the stars in the summer when we were in Maine. And she used to take me to the Planetarium and give me books to read. I've just— I don't know—I've just never thought about doing anything else."

"Okay. Strong influence of grandmother on career," she said out loud as she wrote.

We heard the front door of the apartment bang then, and we heard Bill come in. Mona said something in a low voice, and Bill didn't answer. Then we heard Mona say, louder, "Well, can't you even say hello?"

Still Bill didn't answer. Luisa looked at me and then she looked quickly down at her notebook.

"Frank went out right after breakfast, and he didn't come back for lunch," Mona said.

We heard the sound of a chair being shifted, but still Bill didn't speak.

"Well, don't you care?" Mona asked.

"Why shouldn't he go out if he wants to?" Bill said at last. "I don't blame him." His voice sounded dull and somehow flattened out.

"Doesn't it make any difference to you that your children spend most of their time on the streets?" Mona asked. There was a noise as though Bill had kicked a piece of furniture, but he didn't say anything. "How can you be so unfeeling?" Mona cried, her voice high and shrill. "I've never known anybody so callous as you in my life! Don't you care about anything, anything at all?"

128

Still Bill did not say anything, but we heard him move from one chair to another and the sound of an ashtray banging down on a table.

"All you do is smoke!" Mona cried. "All you care about are those damned cigarettes! The children and I could be murdered before your eyes for all it would matter to you." Oscar barked excitedly. "Oh, get away from me, you loathsome beast," Mona cried.

Luisa bent her head low over her psychiatrist's pad and pretended to be busy writing. But I had seen her face grow flushed when Mona started to scream, and then drain empty of color. Now as her pencil moved jerkily across her pad her face was dead white and her hair blazing as it swung forward over her cheeks. I looked at her and then I looked away and stared up at the underside of the upper bunk.

6

"Even if I can't really explain it," Luisa said in a shaky voice, "I know that what you said is very indicative. Can you tell me something more? Do you remember anything else?"

I lay there on the bottom bunk and the pattern of slats and springs seemed imprinted on my eyes, and I remembered. I remembered something that had been pushed so far back into the dark corners of my mind that until that moment it was almost as though it had been forgotten completely. It was strange that I could manage to forget something so terribly important and yet remember other things. But this new memory I must have pushed back deliberately because it was something I could not bear to remember; I could not remember it and go on living casually and happily each day.

Now the words that Mona screamed at Bill suddenly stirred the cloudy dregs of my mind and sent this bad memory swirling to the foreground. I closed my eyes in order not to feel Luisa looking at me and trying to concentrate on her analysis so that she would not have to hear the words that Mona was throwing at Bill. In the living room Mona's voice went on, but I no longer heard the words because there was in my mind no room for anything but the memory that was now thoroughly roused and thrusting itself upon me.

It was in the summer when we were up in Maine. I must have been four or five. It was the middle of the summer and I remember the feeling of everything being very languid and warm and green. Grandmother Wilding was coming up to spend two weeks with us; Uncle Tod Wilding was driving her up and we expected them around suppertime. All day I kept asking, "When is Grandmother coming? When is Grandmother coming?" and my mother or Binny would answer, "She will be here for your supper."

But suppertime came and my grandmother did not come.

Binny took me upstairs and undressed me and gave me a bath and put on my pajamas and told me to go downstairs and say good night to Mother and Father. I went downstairs and stood in the doorway to the porch and watched my father pouring out two cocktails, one for him and one for Mother. And Mother sat on a green porch rocking chair and rocked back and forth and the tears streamed down her cheeks and

I was afraid to go out to them. Then suddenly my mother leaned forward and wiped away the tears with the back of her hand and said in a shaky, angry voice, "How can you be so unfeeling! Tod and Mama should have been here hours ago, they would have unless . . . and you sit there drinking cocktails as though nothing had happened."

"What do you want me to do?" my father asked, and his face assumed the stony look of one of the statues in the Metropolitan.

"I want you to worry!" my mother cried. "I want you to care that I am worried sick! I know something terrible has— And you just sit there, you just sit there with your cocktail and do nothing! All you care about is your cocktail!"

"There isn't anything I can do, Rose," my father said very quietly. "I've called your mother's house and there wasn't any answer so they must undoubtedly have left. If they haven't arrived by ten o'clock I'll call Marge and Jen, but I don't want to worry them unless absolutely necessary." This was before Aunt Jen married, when she was still living with Uncle Tod and Aunt Marge.

"Oh, my God," my mother said. "Oh, my God."

"Would it make you any happier if I tramped up and down and twisted my face around in agony?" my father asked my mother. "There's nothing to do now but wait and see; and I don't happen to feel that the outward show of anxiety will help matters."

"If you really cared I wouldn't mind," my mother said. "If you were trying to be calm for my sake. But you aren't worried. You just don't care if Tod and Mama . . . it wouldn't matter to you if there's been some terrible accident."

"Aren't you being a little hysterical, Rose?" my father asked. "There are any number of things that may have detained them."

But my mother shook her head. "No, no. You've always been that way. You never worry about anything. You always say, Oh, it will be all right. When Mama had pneumonia you weren't worried, you didn't care."

Very carefully my father poured himself another cocktail; then he said slowly, "Is it because you think I don't like your mother, that men aren't supposed to like their mothers-in-law, that you're talking like this? I assure you that you're wrong. I'm closer to your mother than I ever was to my own."

"No, no," my mother said again. "It isn't just Mama. It's everything. When Camilla had measles last winter and her temperature went to a hundred and six you didn't worry. You just said that she was having the best of care and that all children had to go through— And you didn't worry about me when she was born. Mama said you just sat there reading a book all those hours—all those hours I was in such terrible pain and danger."

"You weren't in any more pain or danger than any

other woman who's had a child," my father said. "Camilla was a perfectly normal delivery without complications."

And my mother cried in great fury, "I can't bear it! I can't bear it! How could any woman bear to live with—to have to see every single day a man who has no feelings—completely callous—"

My father put his glass down on the arm of his chair and walked off the porch and my mother sat there in the rocking chair breathing quickly and rocking back and forth, not crying, but trembling with anger.

I stood in the doorway until Binny called me. "Camilla! Have you said good night to your mother and father?"

Then I went out on the porch and my mother stopped rocking with those little vicious jerks and pulled me up onto her lap and I lay back against her and the flies were buzzing up against the screens, and in the trees the birds were still calling. My mother bent over me and kissed me on my head and cheeks and the back of my neck and then she pushed me off her lap and said, "Run along upstairs to bed now, baby. I'll send Grandmother up to you when she comes."

I went upstairs and Binny put me in bed and pulled down the green shades and kissed me good night and shut the door; but I could not sleep. The last deep yellow rays of the setting sun came in around the blinds and fell in golden shafts on the floor and I lay there in bed and I thought, Grandmother and Uncle

Tod have had a terrible accident. Something dreadful has happened.

I kept thinking this and being frightened, until at last I fell asleep. I was awakened by voices and laughter and I got quickly out of bed and ran to the window. And there in the driveway was Uncle Tod's long, low, open car; and spilling out of it were Grandmother and all the Wildings, Uncle Tod and Aunt Marge and the three kids, Podge and Toddy and Tim, and Aunt Jen with her arms full of packages. And Mother was flinging her arms around Grandmother's neck, and crying, "Oh, Mama, what happened, what happened—we were almost frantic, we—Marjorie, Jenny, children, I'm glad to see you—oh, Mama, we thought something had happened to you and Tod—that there'd been an accident or something!"

"Well, if you will talk on the telephone all day long so no one can reach you," my grandmother said.

"But we haven't used the telephone all day!" my mother cried. "Only when Rafferty called your house to see if you might be still—and there wasn't any answer so we knew you'd left. But that was the only time we used the— Are you sure you called?"

"Am I in the habit of saying I've done things when I haven't, Rose?" my grandmother asked.

My father said to my grandmother, "We're on a party line, you know. It was probably someone else on the line talking whenever you called. The people down the road use the phone for hours at a time."

"But long-distance, wouldn't you think they'd do

135

something about long-distance!" my mother cried, her voice still frantic in the evening air rising up to my room.

Uncle Tod put his arm around her and said, "We're all here, safe and sound. Aren't you going to ask us in for dinner? Now don't worry about food because we've brought a ham, all cooked, and the trunk of the car is piled with things from the garden, and a turkey, too, and you can see that Jen is loaded down with practically the entire A and P."

"Oh, come in, come in," my mother cried, flinging her arms open wide. "Oh, my darlings, I'm so glad to see you all. And you can stay for a whole week! All of you? Oh, that will be so—and Camilla will adore having the children to play with."

"Where's Camilla, where's Camilla?" the children were dinning as they all pushed open the door and went into the house. I ran downstairs then, shouting, "Hello, hello, hello!" with Binny running after me, holding out my slippers.

Aunt Marjorie picked me up and gave me a hug. "Oh, she doesn't need slippers on a warm night like this, do you, elf?" And all the children were dancing up and down and I begged, "May I stay down and eat with you, please, may I?"

My mother said, "What do you think, Raff? Do you think it's all right?"

My father said, "It's entirely up to you, Rose. If you're going to worry about her being up so late by all means send her back upstairs. We've had enough

136

worrying for one day." His voice was low and cold and I could see that he was still very angry with her for the things she'd said to him earlier that evening.

"For the Lord's sake, of course she can stay," Uncle Tod said. "She's a fine, healthy child. Does children good to get off their schedules once in a while. Have two more, Rose, and you won't worry about Camilla nearly as much."

Podge, the oldest of my cousins, said, "Let her stay, please, Aunt Rose. I'll take care of her."

Aunt Jen said, "She can have a long nap tomorrow afternoon."

Somehow all the suitcases got upstairs and the turkey on ice and everybody distributed around the different rooms. My room was a great big room and had two beds, and two folding cots were put up, and I was terribly excited because I was going to sleep in the same room with my wonderful cousins, Podge and Toddy and Tim.

Then we were all downstairs again and Podge and Toddy were busy passing plates with crackers and cheese, and I realized that my father was more than just angry with my mother. He sat on the arm of Aunt Jen's chair and talked and laughed with her and spoke to my mother only when she asked him a direct question, and then he answered it as briefly as possible.

We sat down to dinner and the table in the dining room had all the leaves put in. Aunt Jen sat at my father's right and again he directed all his conversation and all his laughter to her, and she laughed and talked up at him and her eyes were very shiny and it was as though the two of them were in a separate circle of candlelight and everybody else was in the cold and shadow outside. When I looked at my mother at the other end of the table she looked very white and she was talking much too quickly and making jokes and laughing and she did not eat a thing.

After dinner we children were sent to bed. Toddy and Tim fell asleep right away but I couldn't sleep and I heard Podge moving about in the bed next to me so I whispered, "Podge."

And she whispered back, "Can't you sleep?"

"No."

She whispered, "Let's tiptoe downstairs to the landing and sit there and watch. We often do that at home. It's fun."

So we crept downstairs and sat on the landing. We could see the hall very clearly and we could see through the double doors into the living room. They were all sitting around and talking, but after a while my father and Aunt Jen came out into the hall, and Podge nudged me to be very still. My father had his arm about Aunt Jen's waist, and he was looking down at her and smiling and again it seemed that they were in their own separate warm circle of candlelight. They just stood there, my father looking down at Aunt Jen and Aunt Jen looking up at him, and then they went back slowly into the living room again, but my father kept his arm about Aunt Jen.

Podge whispered to me, "I heard my mother tell my

father once that Aunt Jen loved your father and always would." I didn't say anything and after a while Podge whispered. "Gosh, Camilla, but your mother's beautiful. She's like all the princesses in the fairy tales. Aunt Jen isn't anywhere near as pretty as Aunt Rose."

No, I knew that. You would not even know that Aunt Jen and my mother were sisters. Aunt Jen was small and had short curly brown hair and the manner of an interested little sparrow. She was always doing nice things for other people and everybody loved her; but I never caught anybody looking at her the way people have looked at my mother.

Then my mother came out into the hall and just stood there, and after a moment my father came out after her, and said in a low voice, "Well, what do you want?"

My mother said, soft and trembling, "All I want is love and affection, and you don't seem to be able to give me that."

My father still sounded drawn away and angry as he answered, "I told you before I married you that I wasn't demonstrative."

My mother gave a funny little laugh that was somehow terribly forlorn. "I didn't think anybody could carry it to the extremes that you do."

"Well, there it is," my father said.

"You were being affectionate enough with Jen this evening." My mother's voice was low.

"Jen doesn't demand affection," my father said. "It's a lot easier to give it when it isn't clamored for."

"Anyhow, do you think it's fair to Jen?" my mother asked. "The way you've been behaving with her this evening? Quite aside from whether or not it's fair to me?"

"That's up to me to decide." My father made a movement as though to go back to the living room, but my mother stopped him.

"Perhaps if you feel that way about it we should separate," my mother said.

My father's voice sounded cold and indifferent as he answered, "Perhaps we should."

Then into my mother's eyes came a look of shocked terror, of wild animal panic. She drew in her breath sharply. "A little love seems such a small thing to ask," she whispered.

"I'm sorry," my father said.

"Do you think you could love Jen?" my mother asked. "I mean the way I want to be loved?" There was horrible fear in her voice.

"I don't think so," my father said, and he sounded still cold and dull; he turned away from my mother and went back to the living room. My mother fell against the wall and stood leaning there in her white dress, beautiful as a despairing angel. She stood there supported by the wall and she did not cry.

Podge took my hand and then we slipped back upstairs. Podge never said anything about what we had heard, and neither did I. Indeed, until the time that

Uncle Tod moved out West, Podge and I were always awkward and shy together, and I wonder if the eavesdropping was why. The rest of the week the Wildings were with us that summer in Maine, they all played and swam and ate huge meals on the extended dining-room table and it seemed as though Podge and I must have dreamed the bad things that happened, because my mother and father seemed happy and not as though they had said those terrible things to each other.

But I knew it had not been a dream.

Aunt Jen got married and went to Birmingham, Alabama, to live; and after Grandmother died Uncle Tod moved out to California and we hear from them mostly just at Christmas and birthdays.

So there were the two memories and I would have given anything in the world if I could have kept them hidden where they had been for so many years, deep, deep, back in my mind. For now Father was different in my feelings too. Now Father, like Mother, was no longer just my father. He was Rafferty Dickinson, as complete and separate a person as Camilla Dickinson. When I, on that faraway time of my birthday, woke up to the fact that I *was* Camilla Dickinson, I hadn't waked up to the fact that my parents weren't created especially for me, that they were separate people, too, as separate as the people across the court; and it had taken me all this time to realize it and the realization was a deep aching pain. It is a much more upsetting thing to realize that your parents are human beings than it is to realize that you are one yourself. I lay on the bottom bunk of Luisa's bed and it seemed as though a heavy weight were pressing down upon my chest and slowly crushing my heart.

Then in the living room I heard Mona saying, "And what about Frank? Don't you even care that he spends half his time with those cheap Italian girls?"

"What about the Dickinson child?" Bill asked in a bored voice. "I thought she was the new one."

"That spoiled little snit? I'm not sure I don't prefer the Italians. At least they're human."

Luisa looked up from her pad and said deliberately, "Frank went over to Pompilia Riccioli's for lunch. He'll probably stay for supper too. He usually does."

Lying there on her bed, I felt, Oh, no! Life is too difficult, too terrible; how can anybody endure it? And I turned my face to the wall.

"I'm sorry," Luisa said then. "I'm sorry, Camilla. I shouldn't have told you that."

"I don't care," I said.

"And don't mind about Mona. She doesn't mean it. Truly."

"I don't care," I said again. What difference did it make? What difference did it make what Mona thought, or Bill, or Luisa, or anybody? I lay staring up at the slats and I was filled with a fear of Pompilia Riccioli, of the little Italian girls who were at least human. I was filled with a fear of love because of what it had done to my mother and father, of what it had done to Mona and Bill; and the fear seeped through my entire body until I was waterlogged with it, like a piece of driftwood on the beach after a storm.

In the living room Mona screamed suddenly. "Oh, damn the war! Damn it! It's been over for years, why can't it *be* over! Frank spends half his time with that horrible legless creature over on Perry Street and the only time you act human is when you're telling somebody about what you did in the South Pacific. You're not in the South Pacific now. You're in New York. Why can't you forget it? It's over! Why can't you leave it alone?"

"Why can't you leave me alone?" Bill asked.

Luisa banged her pad down on her desk. "Let's get out of here," she said. "Let's take Oscar for a walk or go to a movie or something."

"I can't," I said.

"Why not?"

I didn't want to answer but I said finally, "I'm supposed to see Frank this afternoon."

"Oh, you are? You're a dope if you let yourself be at Frank's beck and call, did you know that, Camilla Dickinson? No man wants any girl he can have as easily as all that."

"I can't help it," I said.

"Aw, come on, Camilla," Luisa urged. "Let's go. Keep him waiting for a few minutes. It'll do him good."

"No, I can't," I said. "I can't."

"You make me sick," Luisa said. "You make me so sick I could vomit."

Then the front door banged and I heard Frank's footsteps and he walked through the living room without speaking to Mona and Bill and came and stood in the doorway to Luisa's room. "Hi."

"Hi," I said.

"What are you doing home?" Luisa asked rudely. "I thought you were out for the day."

"Nope. Got a date with Camilla."

"Camilla's busy."

"No, I'm not," I said.

Luisa turned on me. "You said you were going to spend the day with me."

I shook my head. "I said I'd come down first thing this morning and I did. I've spent the whole morning with you."

"A fat lot I think of anyone who breaks promises," Luisa said.

"I didn't break any promise. I said I'd come and I did."

"I don't mean that," Luisa said scornfully, "and you know it. Don't try playing dumb, Camilla Dickinson. You didn't tell me about Jacques or yesterday afternoon or anything."

"I never promised I'd tell you," I said.

Luisa grew white as she always did when she was angry. "Mona said you were a spoiled little snit who wasn't even human, and she's right. Go on out with

144

Frank if you want to. Do anything you like with him, only don't ever expect my help about anything ever again. As for you, Frank Rowan, I'm surprised to see you rushing about being so social, today of all days."

Although Frank was standing still, when Luisa spoke these words he seemed to give the effect of suddenly stopping. "What do you mean?"

"Don't you know?" Luisa asked, and there was a really nasty grin on her face.

Frank seemed to grow stiller and stiller. "It would be a good idea if you would shut up," he said.

"As a psychiatrist I was just curious to see how you'd be," Luisa said, "but I can't say it's seemed to bother you any."

Then Frank broke away and grabbed me by the arm. "Come on, Camilla," he said, "let's get out of here." He dragged me from the apartment. When we got out on the street we stopped to catch our breaths and Frank said, quite calmly, as though there had not been this enormous Thing between him and Luisa just a few moments before, "I should think Mona and Bill provide enough scenes so Luisa wouldn't want to add to them." Still holding my arm, he started walking rapidly up the street, and I walked along beside him and we said nothing until he led me into a drugstore.

"I thought we'd have a cup of hot chocolate," he said, "even if it isn't very cold. I thought it would taste good anyhow. Hot chocolate always goes with November to me. Oh, listen, have you had any lunch?"

"No."

"You'd better have a sandwich and some soup, then. What kind of a sandwich?"

"Oh, I don't care. Anything. Lettuce, tomato, and bacon, I guess."

Frank ordered for me and I was worried. Worried about the things he and Luisa had said and worried because I didn't know whether he got any more allowance than Luisa or not, and I thought he probably didn't. And he'd paid for the movie the night before. I wanted to offer to pay for my food but I was afraid it would make him angry.

But then he said, "I've got a job, Camilla. I'm tutoring the son of one of Mona's friends in Latin at fifty cents an hour. So from now on I'll have a few bits of silver to rub against each other in my pocket. Not much, but we can do a couple of things together. Listen, this astronomy business. How serious is it with you?"

"Completely serious," I said.

"Well, tell me something, then," he demanded as my soup and sandwich were put in front of me.

"Tell you what?" I asked blankly.

"What do you do about it? I mean to prepare yourself."

"I read. I study mathematics. An astronomer has to have a terrific foundation of mathematics."

Frank nodded. "That's true enough." And then he took a swallow of his hot chocolate and he seemed to go miles and miles away from me. I put my hands around my cup and my fingers were cold and the warmth was comforting.

Then Frank said, "I hadn't forgotten—what Luisa said. I just didn't want to talk about it. Not even to David. I'd like you to meet David, Cam. He's twenty-seven. Exactly ten years older than I am. He's the best friend I have in the world. Was your father in the war, Cam?"

"He did camouflage."

"Did he go overseas?"

"He was in France for a while."

"Bill went to the Pacific. Mona and Bill don't like me going to see David. They think it's neurotic. It's not neurotic. I don't go to see David because he lost his legs. I go see him because he's just a wonderful person, and the wisest one I know. Has Luisa talked to you any about David?"

"No," I said, and in spite of my pity I felt a pang of jealousy for this David who took up so much of Frank's time and thought.

"Luisa came with me once to see him but they didn't like each other. Luisa always asks too many questions. The wrong kind of questions. David has a pair of artificial legs he wears when he goes to the park, but he can't ever wear them to walk with because he was wounded in the stomach too. I don't exactly know why, but it would put too much strain on his stomach for him to use artificial legs." Then Frank stopped and looked at me. "You wouldn't be afraid to see him, Camilla?"

"No," I said.

"Luisa was. With all her talk about being a doctor, she was afraid. I think that's why they didn't get on, why she said all the wrong things. The thing is, though, when you're with David you don't think of anything but *David*. You don't think about his legs."

No, for some reason I was not afraid at the prospect of meeting David. I knew that Frank would never take me to see anyone like David in order to frighten me, as Luisa might possibly have done.

"Okay. We'll go there next weekend. Listen, let's walk."

When we walked we never seemed to talk. We walked in silence to the Square and sat down on one of the benches. Frank began to speak as though suddenly the silence was bothering him and he had to fill it with words. "I used to want to be a pianist. But you have to be a lot younger than I am really to get anywhere. And sometimes I think I would like to be a scholar. I love curious facts. Do you know how Aeschylus died? An eagle dropped a tortoise on his head. And Alborak was the name of the white mule Mohammed went to heaven on. But now I think I'd better be a doctor."

"Like Luisa?" I asked.

"No. Not like Luisa. I don't know exactly why Luisa wants to be a doctor, but she talks about it in such an odd way that I know it's not for my reason."

"What's your reason?"

"A very simple one. To be a doctor is to be on the

side of life. I'm against death. I resent it. I want to do everything I can against it." Then he said, as though everything else he had said since we had left the apartment had been a painful preliminary:

"Camilla, I—I have to go see the Stephanowskis. I—I was being a coward. I didn't want to go today. But I have to."

"All right," I said.

"Camilla, maybe one reason I like you so much is that you're so different from Luisa. Luisa would have been all full of questions, but you just wait." He looked down at a pigeon picking up some Cracker Jacks that had been spilled on the walk.

"It's about Johnny," he said. "Johnny Stephanowski. He was my best friend. I haven't ever talked to anybody about him. Not to Luisa. Or Mona or Bill. Only David a little but not much because he—somehow he doesn't quite understand the way I feel about Johnny even though he does about everything else." He stopped talking for a moment; his teeth were clenched and the line of his jaw was tight and strained.

"We've only really known each other since Thursday, me and the Stephanowskis—but time doesn't have anything to do with it." He stopped, and his silence was louder than words. Then he said, "Johnny and I were real friends. Not kid stuff. Real friends. I knew him since we were kids. His mother and father own the store where Mona buys all her records. I never knew his parents very well. Johnny and I always had too much to do to be bothered with older people.

Then last year when Mona and Bill sent me off to school, the Stephanowskis sent Johnny too. It meant a lot to them, sending Johnny away to a prep school. It was—I don't think you could understand how important it was to them, Camilla. It was as though—as though they were opening some kind of door for him. At least they thought about it that way. We had a wonderful time at school. The kids all liked us and we were both good at football and baseball but even when there was a gang of us kidding around or something it was still Johnny and me. We used to sneak off at the end of study hall into the chapel and listen to Mr. Mitchell, the music master, practicing the organ. He knew we did it, but he was a good egg and never reported us. We used to lie stretched out on the wooden pews and listen to him playing *Wachet auf, ruft uns die Stimme*, *O Bone Jesu*, the *St. Matthew Passion*. I think maybe that's why I'm not like Luisa or Mona or Bill. About God, I mean. You know, Cam, you could actually feel the pulse of the music vibrating through your body from the boards of the pew. I listened with my body as well as with my ears, and everything seemed clear and wonderful, God and man and the universe, and I thought everything would be all right because I had books and music and Johnny and when I was at school, away from Mona and Bill and the apartment, I could forget about how awful they are to each other, and see them in my mind loving each other, the way people who are married ought to. The way the Stephanowskis do. They really do, Cam, in spite of—in spite of everything. Johnny's older brother—the one who knew David—died in the war. Now there're only the two kids, Pete and Wanda. People oughtn't to have to die, Cam. There's something awfully unfair about being born if you're going to have to die. It's like being born knowing you have a fatal illness. Johnny—"

He paused for a long time, staring down at a squirrel busily eating a peanut.

Then at last he said, "One of the kids on our hall got hold of a gun. Of course they weren't allowed and he kept it hidden. Johnny was crazy about guns and he went over to look at this one and it went off." He paused again, a long moment of black silence. Then he said, so low that I could scarcely hear, so that I almost had to guess at his words, "He didn't die right away. He kept saying 'Frank, Frank, Frank,' over and over and they let me stay with him. Cam, I don't see how anyone can see someone die and ever be the same again."

He stopped talking completely and this time the silence had a finished quality to it; it was the complete white silence that comes after a snowfall. We sat there on the bench and the squirrel scurried up a tree and the pigeon picked up a last piece of Cracker Jack and then flew off clumsily over the grass. It was almost as though Frank's words about death had sent them away from us, fleeing to the safety of little girls playing hopscotch and nurses knitting as they sat by sleeping babies in baby carriages.

I don't know how long we sat there, not talking, but when Frank spoke again his voice had lost that frightening quality of death, and I wanted to call to the squirrel and the pigeon: It's all right now, you can come back.

"I got kicked out of a school a few weeks after that," Frank said. "I'll tell you about it sometime. I'd seen the Stephanowskis when they came up after—after Johnny, but when I got back to New York it was a long time before I went to see them. I didn't want to talk about Johnny to anyone, and I thought they might want me to. Then Mona made me go over to buy some records—and then I just got into the habit of seeing them. I had the—the effrontery to think that I might help them, but they were the ones who helped me. If you don't mind, let's go over there now. Johnny died a year ago today. Snow's late this year. It was snowing this time last year."

Then he said very softly, "Johnny was alive all the time, you see. That's what I don't understand. I don't understand how Johnny could be stopped when he wasn't ready to be stopped. It isn't fair, it isn't right! Johnny was just beginning, everything was still in front of him; he had so much that he wanted to do and he didn't get a chance to do any of it. It's wrong, Camilla, it's horrible!" His voice was very loud and excited.

Then he said more quietly, "Camilla, you're the only person I've been able to talk to about this. I couldn't talk to the Stephanowskis because of course having Johnny die was much more terrible for them than for me. It's helped to be able to say it out loud in words for you. Is it okay about going to the Stephanowskis? I mean, will you go with me?"

"Yes," I said.

We walked slowly to the music shop and this time the silence was all right. It was the kind of silence that you find in the country and on quiet streets in early evening, a kind of silence that is complete and full in itself and has no need to be broken because there is nothing that needs to come out of it. The silence itself said everything that needed to be said between us.

The music shop was empty when we went in and a gray-haired man and woman were sitting behind the counter. The woman came around the counter and put her arms round Frank, and just said, "Franky, Franky," and kissed him as though she were his mother.

Frank kissed her and just said, "Hi, Mrs. Stephanowski," and then he shook Mr. Stephanowski's hand and then he said, "This is Camilla. I brought her today because I want you to know her."

They both looked at me and I felt somehow that what they thought of me was terribly important and I was filled with relief when Mrs. Stephanowski smiled and took my hand in hers. Some customers came in then and Mr. Stephanowski said, "Take Camilla into one of the booths and give her a concert if you feel like it, Franky."

"Thanks, Mr. Stephanowski," Frank said. "I'd like

to." He picked out an album and we went into the last of the small listening booths. Frank had me sit down in the chair. "Do you know Holst's *The Planets?*" he asked.

I shook my head. "No. What is it?"

"It's kind of queer," Frank told me, "but it's kind of wonderful. I thought maybe it might be interesting to you. Of course it isn't scientific or anything, but I think it's sort of interesting to listen to a musician's conception of stars. There's one place that sounds to me like the noise the planets must make grinding against space."

He put the record on and it was different from anything I knew. I knew Bach and Beethoven and Brahms and Chopin and I loved them, especially Bach; but this music—it was like stars before you understand them, when you think an astronomer is an astrologer, when they are wild, distant, mysterious things. And as I listened I realized that the music had a plan to it, that none of the conflicting notes came by accident.

"Why haven't I heard this before!" I cried, and Frank smiled at me and changed the record. When he smiled, his face lit up in a way that I have never seen Luisa's light up, and he seemed to me completely beautiful.

When *The Planets* was finished, Frank said, "What next, Camilla? You choose something."

But I shook my head. "I'd rather listen to something you like particularly."

"Well," Frank said, "I have a game I play. I have

154

music for everybody. That was Johnny's idea, doing that, and now David and I do it too. I'll play yours." He went out into the shop, where several customers were now gathered about the counter, and came back with another album.

"What is it?" I asked.

"Prokofiev's Third Piano Concerto. Particularly the andantino. You probably won't think it sounds like you." His voice was suddenly gruff and embarrassed.

I listened and it didn't sound to me like me, but it was as exciting and different as *The Planets* had been, and as I listened I was filled with a great tremendous excitement. Oh, I love I love I love! I cried inside myself. So many people, so many things! Music and stars and snow and weather! Oh, if one could always feel this warm love, this excitement, this glory of the infinite possibilities of life!

And as I listened to the music I knew that everything was possible.

"I think that's enough for a start," Frank said, and we went back into the shop. As Frank put the records back on the shelves Mrs. Stephanowski excused herself from a customer.

"Franky, you'll come for dinner tonight?"

"Sure," Frank said. "Sure, yes."

"And you, Camilla? Could you come along maybe? It would be a pleasure for us to have you. Maybe Franky's said something to you about Johnny, but don't let that—I wouldn't want to ask just anyone over tonight but I'd like to ask you."

"Thank you," I said. "I'd love to. But I'll have to ask my parents."

She pushed the telephone over to me and I dialed. Carter answered, so I told her to ask Mother if I could stay out to dinner. There was silence and then Carter told me that my mother wanted me to come home.

"Let me speak to Mother," I asked.

But Carter said in that voice of hers that never has any more warmth than a goldfish, "Your mother doesn't feel very well, Miss Camilla. I don't want to disturb her again. She said you was to come home and I think you'd better. It's time you learned some consideration."

"Let me speak to Mother, please," I said again, but she had hung up on me.

Mrs. Stephanowski put her hand on my shoulder. "If your mother wants you home you run along. Franky'll bring you over another time. I'm glad Franky brought you in. You're a nice girl. Pretty too. Good for him. Bring her in soon, Franky."

"I will," Frank said. "I'll take you home, Cam. See you in about an hour, Mrs. Stephanowski."

When we reached my apartment building Frank said, "Listen, you can get all your weekend homework done tonight, can't you?"

"Yes."

"Then I'll meet you at the obelisk at ten tomorrow morning. Okay?"

"Okay," I said.

He gave me a quick handshake and left me and I went into the apartment building. Neither the doorman nor the elevator boy said anything to me beyond "Good afternoon, Miss Camilla," but it seemed to me from the way they looked at me that Jacques must be there and I wanted to run out of the house and race down the street after Frank.

But when I got into the apartment Mother was lying in bed looking at a magazine and she kissed me and sent for Carter to bring in some tea for us.

"Who were you with all day?" she asked.

"Luisa and Frank."

"Frank?"

"Luisa's brother."

"You haven't talked about Frank much."

"I've only been seeing him lately," I said.

"Did you come home alone?" she asked me.

"No. Frank brought me."

"Do you—do you like him?"

"More than anybody I've ever met," I said, and it seemed that I was still walking through the streets with Frank instead of standing by my mother's bed. "I have to do my homework now," I said. "Will Father be home for dinner?"

"Yes," Mother said, and reached out for my hand. "Oh, Camilla, you're such a clam. And you used to be such a warm, affectionate little girl. What is it? What happened to you?"

"Nothing," I said. I left Mother and went into my room and did my homework. Then I called Luisa, but

157

she wouldn't speak to me, and I was angry with her for being angry with me. My father came home and I sat with him while he had his cocktail, but neither of us talked. And all I wanted in the world was to go to the park and wait by the obelisk till morning.

7

On Sundays both my parents had breakfast late so I ate alone in the kitchen and then went to the park and to the obelisk. It was too early for Frank to be there and I watched some children playing Giant Steps up and down the obelisk steps. I felt terribly old. A year ago I was still sometimes playing Giant Steps with the children in the park, but now I just stood there and watched them. I knew then that I had lived longer since last Wednesday than all the rest of my life added together. You can add up the same number of days and get different answers: two and two does not make four. Even the truth of mathematics is variable. I sighed, and a sailor walked by and whistled at me.

Frank was early too. I hadn't been there long when he came up and said, "Hello, Camilla."

I said, "Hello, Frank."

He asked me, "How are you this morning?"

And I answered, "I don't know," even though I was afraid it might sound like a silly answer; but I felt that I must always be honest with Frank.

He just said, "I don't know how I am, either, so that makes two of us."

We started to walk together, not touching, but very close, and Frank asked me, "Did you like the Stephan-owskis?"

"Yes," I said. "More than I've liked anybody since I met Luisa and you."

"They liked you too," Frank said. "They liked you a lot. And they don't like just anybody."

"Frank," I said, "they've had such terrible things happen to them—I mean Johnny and the other one who was killed in the war—and they seemed so—so alive. If anything awful happens to me, then I feel dead—but they were so alive. Being alive is the only way to be happy. And they seemed happy."

"I know," Frank said. "I know exactly what you mean, Cam. Listen, if you look at the people walking past us here in the park, I bet more than half of them have had some awful tragedy in their lives. I don't expect you can live to be very old without having someone you love die. And all kinds of other dreadful things. And I think it's whether you go on staying alive or not that makes you what kind of a person you are. I think it's terribly important to be alive. There are so many dead people walking about, people who might as well be dead for all they care about life, I mean. Mona may be awful, but she's alive. She's never stopped caring about things. I don't think Bill cares much anymore. When Mona throws something at him he throws something back at her, but not because he really means it, just out of habit. That's why I got so mad at you in the movies the other night. I think if you can't stay alive all the way inside you, no matter what happens, then you're betraying life and you might as well be dead."

"Yes," I said. "You were right to be mad at me." And suddenly I became really aware that the sun was shining on us and that the bare branches of the trees looked beautiful against the sky, and Frank was walking beside me and we were together.

Everywhere there were people walking in couples and mothers and fathers pushing baby carriages and I wondered if I ever would walk in Central Park pushing a baby carriage of my own and I suddenly felt terribly old and grown-up, maybe the way Luisa thinks I ought to feel all the time. And I thought, Alma Potter's always talking about the dates she has: I wonder if she'd think this is a date? And I wondered, too, if Alma Potter talked to the boys she went on dates with the way Frank and I talked. It couldn't be as nice, I thought, it couldn't possibly be as exciting. None of the boys I knew, at dancing school or anywhere, talked at all like Frank; but maybe if Frank went to dancing school he wouldn't talk the way he did with me in the park either.

We walked toward the zoo and Frank told me, "Mona had a friend once who came over from Africa. She stayed at the Sherry-Netherland and she thought she was going out of her mind because she was waked up every morning at sunrise by the lions crying, just as though she were still in Kenya. Mona was awfully worried about her, and tried to get her to go to a psychiatrist. Then one day they were talking about it in front of Bill and he laughed and said it was probably the lions at the zoo. And it was."

We laughed loudly, both of us, at the idea of the woman on her vacation from Kenya being awakened each morning by the lions just as though she had never left Africa; and the thought of being awakened by lions in the middle of New York City was somehow a wonderful thing to me.

"I told you I'd tell you how I got kicked out of school," Frank said. "You want to hear it? It's kind of a Thing."

"Yes."

"I mean I don't want to bore you or anything."

Now the sun went behind the clouds and suddenly it was cold and it felt like winter. I drew closer to Frank.

"You wouldn't bore me," I said.

We walked through the zoo to the lion house. Most of the lions were outside, but one lay in his cage, at the very back, curled up in a tawny and miserable heap, and I wondered if such a lion calling from his cage could sound anything like a lion in the wilds of

Africa, if the sound of his crying reaching the Sherry-Netherland across Fifth Avenue could sound like a cry reaching a farm in Kenya across the African veld. Or is it velds they have in Kenya? I've rather forgotten my African geography.

We left the lion house and went and stood in front of a cage of monkeys with their tragic little faces, and Frank said, "At school we used to have chapel every morning and evening and all kinds of stuff. Until Johnny died it was okay. It didn't bother me any. I mean, it didn't really mean much to any of us one way or another. The times I believed in God, I mean really, so it was important to me, was listening to Mr. Mitchell play the organ the way I told you, and then when Johnny and I went on walks, here in New York or at school, if we saw something beautiful, the way the stars look in winter when they first start to break through the daylight and the sky is that sort of greeny blue and the trees are like a charcoal drawing—I could feel God then. Maybe it was just what Mona calls a sentimental pantheism, but it seemed to me it was more than that. When do you feel God most, Camilla?"

"When I'm working with the stars, and when I'm with you." I hesitated a small moment before I said this last. "I've never talked about God to anybody before."

"Not to your parents?"

"No, not really. Not this way."

"For an atheist Mona talks about God an awful lot.

She's always getting me into arguments and discussions. And I think she understood how I felt about Johnny, the horrible stupid wrongness of it, more than anybody else. Bill said the only way to get on in the world is to be so that nothing, no matter how terrible it is, really matters. He said nothing really *does* matter in the long run, so why should we let it bother us."

"But if things don't matter, then you might as well be dead," I said.

"Sure," Frank said. "That's what I mean. That's what I mean all the time. That's what I meant when I got so sore at you that night in the movies. Mona knows things matter anyhow. She said it was a stinking brutal waste and no God worthy of the name would let things like that happen. Well, I think she's wrong there too. It wasn't God's fault the gun went off. If it was God's fault, then we're pulling Him down to the—to our own level. It's like what you said, Cam. It isn't God's fault if we're dopes. But that's what I got kicked out for."

"What do you mean?"

"Well, in chapel after Johnny died the headmaster preached a sort of sermon about it. He said it was God's will that Johnny was taken and all that kind of junk. You know what I mean."

I nodded.

Again Frank's voice rose and soared as it always did whenever he cared tremendously about something. "If I thought God made that gun go off, if I thought God willed Johnny to die, I wouldn't believe in Him. I'd do everything in my power to obliterate His name from the face of the earth. But I *don't* believe it! I'll be damned rather than believe it. And I mean that, absolutely and literally."

I nodded again, and I wanted to cry out for joy, Oh, yes! Yes! We believe in the same God! And the fact that Frank and I believed in the same God seemed to clear me for the moment of all confusion and make me strong and unafraid. But how could I cry out for joy when Frank was still torn with the agony of Johnny's death?

"I walked out of chapel while he was still talking," Frank said. "I got up and stalked down the aisle and slammed the chapel door. I didn't even know I was doing it until I was upstairs in my room. I don't expect they would have expelled me just for that. They said I was too upset to know what I was doing and they put me in the infirmary overnight and gave me something to make me sleep and it gave me a vile headache the next morning.

"Then what happened?" I asked.

"The headmaster called me into his office the next day and tried to talk to me. He said he was trying to comfort me. So I told him there wasn't any point, we simply didn't believe in the same God. And he said there was only one God and you either believed in Him or you didn't and I said nobody knew what God was anyhow and he was trying to make God in his own image instead of the other way around, the way it ought to be, and then he went on about how I was unbearably arrogant. Maybe I was. But if I had to believe in his God instead of mine I'd have got hold of that gun somehow and shot myself then and there. He went on talking a lot of bilge and I just did my best not to listen and then he said Okay, you're still too upset about Johnny to know what you're thinking or saying, we'll forget the whole matter for a few weeks until you're feeling more yourself and then we'll have another talk. So he waited a few weeks and we had another talk and he said anybody who felt about things the way I did wouldn't be happy in his school and he made a few cracks about my having liked Johnny too much anyhow so I walked out of his office like I did out of chapel and took the next train home. The kids all went down to the train to see me off. It raised quite a stink. What a dope that guy was. The other fellows were all okay. They didn't go around trying to comfort me. They were just there, cracking jokes and making me laugh and getting up extra baseball practice. And Mr. Mitchell too. He went around organizing hikes and once when I went into the chapel at the end of study hall to listen to him play the organ he got up and said, 'Come on, Rowan, and I'll show you how this thing works,' and gave me an organ lesson. I suppose it was all my own dumb fool fault, really, the whole business of getting kicked out. But I didn't care much one way or another. I'm kind of sorry now. It was just an easy way out. Mona gave me hell and she was right. Johnny'd probably have had fits too. He always said I was trying to use my mind too much about God. Maybe I do, but it's the only thing I know how to use." He stopped and grabbed hold of the bars of the elephant's fence. The elephant lumbered over to a bucket of mash, put in his trunk, fed himself a mouthful, and then looked at us with his tiny, ancient-looking eyes, and blew bubbles.

Frank roared with laughter. The elephant looked at us again, batted his gray wrinkled lids in a coquettish manner, turned around and offered us his rear.

I laughed, too, and we stood there, holding on to the bars and shaking with wild laughter.

Then, when we had controlled ourselves, I said, "It was sort of like Galileo. You, I mean."

"Only Galileo recanted."

"He shouldn't have. Lots of other people didn't. Martyrs and things."

"I don't want to be a martyr," Frank said. "I just want to live forever. Don't you want to live forever, Camilla?"

"Yes." The elephant moved away from us and lumbered back indoors, his gray skin loose and wrinkled and more like an artificial covering than part of a living body.

"Oh, Frank," I said, "oh, Frank, I'm glad you were expelled. Maybe if you hadn't been you'd have been back there this year instead of in New York."

"Instead of in Central Park Zoo with you." Frank took my arm. "I'm glad too."

That was a funny week, the week that came after that. I didn't see too much of Frank. It was as though we had to have time to breathe between our meetings. I didn't see too much of anybody except Luisa, and I felt I owed it to her. I had breakfast with Father each morning and then left for school early. And after school I either went down to Ninth Street with Luisa to do homework or she came back up with me. Mother and Father didn't go out to dinner once that week, but twice Luisa and I went to drugstores for a sandwich and a milkshake.

Tuesday afternoon I met Frank after school and we went to the Stephanowskis and listened to Bach. I wanted to go to the opera with Frank and to Carnegie Hall. Mother and I went to concerts often on Sunday afternoons, but I felt that the music would sound somehow different and bigger if I heard it with Frank.

I saw Frank Wednesday on the subway but he didn't see me. I was on my way down to Luisa's and at one of the stops a gang of boys got on. They had their arms full of shabby schoolbooks (why do boys' schoolbooks always look so much more dilapidated than girls'?) and they were shouting and laughing as I have seen boys do on subways and buses hundreds of times and I didn't pay any attention to them until the doors started to close and they jammed themselves between the doors, holding them open, and shouting at an unseen companion to hurry, hurry! Then a tall skinny boy with dark red hair pushed his way, panting and laughing, through the door, and it was Frank.

The gang of them (there were only four but they made so much noise it seemed like a gang) were horsing about. They weren't paying any attention to anybody else in the car though they seemed to me to be conscious of having an audience; it was almost as though they were giving a performance. They pushed out ahead of me at the Eighth Street stop and I was almost glad Frank hadn't seen me, he seemed so completely different from the Frank I so far knew, so many millions of years older than I; the Frank who talked to me about God and life and death, who taught me so much more than I already knew about music, how you can single out and listen to the different instruments in an orchestra, and how music feeds your soul when it is hungry the way food does your body. But this Frank I had seen on the subway was just a kid like any other kid.

I went on up to Luisa's and Mona had come home early from work and had sent Luisa to the drugstore for some aspirin. She was sitting on the sofa reading and she told me to sit down and wait till Luisa got back. It was during the week so she wasn't drunk, though she had a drink on the table in front of her.

"Do you like to read?" she asked me, looking up from her book and peering at me through her black-rimmed glasses.

"Yes."

"Luisa and Frank read too much, too many things. I imagine your reading is more appropriate for a child, isn't it?"

"I don't know."

"Ever read Sir Thomas Browne?"

"No."

"Frank gave me this to read. Listen: 'Man is a Noble Animal, splendid in ashes, and pompous in the grave, solemnizing Nativities and Deaths with equal lustre, nor omitting ceremonies of bravery in the infamy of his nature. Life is a pure flame, and we live by an invisible sun within us.' What do you think of that, hah?"

"I think it's beautiful," I said.

"Too many of us let our suns go out." Mona took off her glasses, looked at me without them, and put them on again. "The main thing is to care. As long as you care, your sun hasn't gone out. Though sometimes you can care so much, you can desire so much more than you can ever reach, that your burning sun can consume you utterly. However, that seems to me to be the better fate, because I still happen to think that man is a noble animal. Do you know what I'm talking about? You ought to know. Luisa says you want to be an astronomer. Anybody who wants something ought to know what I'm talking about."

"Yes," I said. "I think I know."

Luisa came in then and we went into her room to do our homework. That night Frank phoned me and we planned that I should meet him Saturday morning down at his house.

During that week Mother was very quiet and she looked tired and unhappy. Carter told me that the days I went down to Luisa's after school Mother went out in the afternoon; but the days I came back from school to the apartment with Luisa she was always there waiting for us with hot chocolate and little cakes, and Jacques did not come. But I still had that dead feeling in my heart when I thought about her and when I was with her. My father was very gentle with her, and twice I saw him go up to her and put his arms around her. Oh, Father, I thought. Oh, Father. And I wanted always to keep him from knowing that Mother had talked to Jacques on the telephone.

It's a funny thing how it takes your emotions much longer than your intellect to realize it when some big change happens in your life. My feeling this new numb way about my parents was the biggest change that had ever happened to me and I couldn't get used to it. All that week I'd wake up in the morning and know that something was wrong and my mind had to tell my heart that it was because my mother had talked to Jacques on the phone, because my parents were Rose and Rafferty Dickinson instead of just Mother and Father. Then my heart would try to adjust itself to unhappiness, but still it didn't realize why it was unhappy and it instinctively turned to Mother for comfort, and then my mind would say, "No, you mustn't do that anymore." And gradually my heart began to know what my mind had been telling it every day: that everything was changed, that nothing could ever be the same again.

Several times during that week I caught Mother and Father looking at me in an odd sort of way and I was worried because I felt that I was making them unhappy. Once at dinner I tried to explain it by making up some sort of excuse, and of course I said completely the wrong thing and made everything worse. We were having salad and Mother was toying with a piece of lettuce on the end of her fork. She looked very lovely in the candlelight and usually when I look at Mother and she seems particularly beautiful it's all I can do to keep myself in my seat when all I want to do is rush around the table and throw my arms about her. But this night I just looked at her and thought how lovely she was, but in a cold intellectual way. I looked at her and she pleased me, but she gave me less personal pleasure than a beautifully solved problem in mathematics would have. And then I noticed that she was looking at me again and my father was looking at me, and I said, "I guess I'm growing up, and when children grow up they don't need their parents the way they used to."

My mother burst into tears and said, "Camilla, what a terrible thing to say!"

Then I did run around to her because I'd meant to

make them happier by explaining it all as a natural process and instead I'd made it worse. I put my arms around her and again it was as though she were the child and I the mother, and I hated it.

Thursday Luisa and I went up to the Metropolitan Museum to do our homework in the Roman garden, where we had first talked. Luisa didn't know the museum very well before she met me. She'd always lived down in the Village and played in Washington Square. I think she missed a lot, not having the Metropolitan to play in. Sometimes three or four of us would slip away from our nurses and steal into the museum and play hide-and-seek until one of the guards caught us and threw us out. The guards hated us and we used to think of them as our enemies and think of all kinds of ways to pester them. I suppose we were horrible, but it was fun and we never hurt anything. But I still feel guilty and as though I oughtn't to be there whenever I see a guard looking at me.

When Luisa and I finished our homework we put our books under our arms and began to wander about looking with half an eye at pictures, statues, urns, beads. When I was little I used to pretend that the museum was a great enormous palace and I was a princess who lived there. I liked best the more deserted rooms, where I could really feel I was just wandering around my home and the guards were my footmen instead of enemies. The museum is a wonderful place to dream. In the rooms with the statues there is a whiteness to the light like the whiteness that comes from freshly fallen snow, only somehow it is snow in a dream and not snow as it is on the street and in the park. And the statues and busts are like something out of a dream, staring and staring at you with their milky, blind eyes.

Luisa stopped in front of a modernistic woman, done in sleek angular black. "What are you doing Saturday, Camilla?" she asked.

"I'm going out with Frank."

"Did he ask you?"

"Of course."

"When?"

"He telephoned me."

"Oh," Luisa said. Her face grew dark and angry; but all she said was, "I suppose it's your right if you want to."

"Yes," I said. "It is." Then again I tried to explain, looking hard at the bas-relief of a Grecian horse. "Luisa, if only you wouldn't get mad when I see Frank—it doesn't make anything different with us because I see Frank. You never mind if I spend the afternoon with one of the other girls from school or if they ask me out to supper—"

"I don't mind if you see Frank," Luisa said.

"Then why do you get mad?"

"I don't get mad," Luisa said.

I turned away because it seemed to me that there

wasn't anything else to say. But Luisa came over to me and touched me softly on the shoulder.

"Camilla—"

"What?"

"Do you remember, long ago, just after we'd first met, and I told you I didn't believe in God, and you were so shocked?"

"Yes."

"And you made me promise to say my prayers at night?"

"Yes."

"Well, I still do it."

"Do you, Luisa? Do you really?"

"Yes. Only it doesn't do any good. When it's a starry night I look up at the stars the way you told me to and try to feel God, but I never do."

"There aren't enough stars in the city," I told her. "You can't see enough stars to get the feeling I meant. They have to be country stars, a whole sky full of them. Then you'd feel what I mean."

"When we went to Fire Island for a week last summer there were plenty of stars then," Luisa said. "And I didn't feel what you meant. I'd like to believe in God, Camilla, but I can't quite seem to."

"Then why do you go on praying?" I asked.

Luisa shook her head unhappily. "It's sort of come to be a superstition with me, I guess. I keep thinking that maybe if there is a God, in spite of everything I ought to keep on praying just in case. I figure it can't do any harm and maybe there's a wild chance it might do some good. But if there is a God he hasn't answered any of my prayers. I pray the same thing every night. It's not like prayers with wishes, I guess. You aren't supposed to tell a wish, but I guess it's all right to tell a prayer. I pray that things will be all right with Mona and Bill, and I pray that I may be just a little pretty." Then she laughed. "Oh, well, laugh, drink, and be merry. As long as you can laugh at it you're all right. *Toujours gai, toujours gai*, that's me." And we started up one of the back staircases hung with huge, dim pictures.

Then Luisa stopped at the curve of the stair and turned on me with the eagerness with which she always starts a new train of thought. "Listen, Camilla, when did you first learn about the per—the perfidy —of adults?" She grinned. "Good word, isn't it?"

"I'm not sure I know what you mean," I said with caution.

"Oh, you know." Luisa shook her head impatiently and continued up the stairs and on into a room hung with enormous paintings by Whistler and Sargent and Homer and people like that. "About adults not being omnipotent. About them not being perfect. About them being like that Bible quote Mona's always throwing about. What is it? Oh, yes. 'The heart is deceitful above all things, and desperately wicked.' Well, that's not exactly what I mean. But when were you first *betrayed* by an adult? Do you remember?"

"Yes," I said.

"Of course, you're such a dope about adults; you don't even realize they're nothing but people. I wondered if you'd remember anything."

"I remember," I said.

"Well, go on. When was it? Where was it?" She sat down on a round bench in the center of the room and pulled me down beside her.

"It was at school," I said. "It must have been around second or third grade because it was a school that only went to third grade."

"Well, go on," Luisa said. "Who was it? What happened?"

I began to feel rather embarrassed, but I knew that Luisa wouldn't let me get this far without finishing.

Mother had come for me that day instead of Binny. She was late, as usual. She rushed at me where I was sitting waiting for her in the coatroom and gave me a kiss and a hug. "I'm sorry I'm late, sweetheart, I— Get your coat and let's hurry." Then, "Camilla, what's the matter with you?"

I bowed my head in shame. "I'm wet," I whispered. "Mother, I wet my pants."

"How did that happen?"

"It was in geography. I had to go to the bathroom and I asked to be excused."

"But, darling, what happened, why—"

"Miss Mercer said I couldn't go. And I had to go awful bad so I asked her again and she said no. And I really had to go, Mother, it wasn't just to get out of class. So I asked her again and she got awfully mad. And I had to go, Mother, I had to, so finally I just got up and ran and I got as far as the bathroom door and then I just went, I just couldn't wait any longer. And then the bell rang and it was time for French and I went back to the classroom."

"All right, darling. Don't worry about it," Mother said.

"But I'm too big to wet my pants," I grieved.

"You wait here just a minute longer, sweetheart. No, you'd better come with me." She took me by the hand and we almost ran to the principal's office. Mother told her what had happened.

"But I can't believe it!" the principal exclaimed.

"I assure you it's true," Mother said.

The principal rang a bell. "I believe Miss Mercer's still here. We'd better send for her and clear the matter up."

Miss Mercer listened with her face like a codfish's while Mother told her my story. Then she said briskly, "What nonsense. She never asked to be excused."

The principal nodded. "You see."

My mother was beginning to get excited. "No, I'm afraid I don't see. Camilla's in the habit of telling the truth and if she says she asked to be excused, then she did."

"Well," Miss Mercer said, "I'm sure I would have let her go if only she'd asked me. Of course a number of children have been using the bathroom as an excuse to leave class, but if a child really has to leave I'm sure I wouldn't keep her. Camilla's probably ashamed of wetting her pants, a big girl like that, and just made up a story to tell you. Her English teacher says she's very imaginative."

"But her imagination does not run to lies and she's no coward," my mother said, her voice like a furious echo of my father's.

Then the principal turned to me. "Camilla, did you have to leave the room during geography?"

I nodded.

"Why didn't you ask Miss Mercer if you could leave?"

"But I did!" I cried. "I asked her three times."

Miss Mercer shrugged. "You see?"

"Camilla," the principal went on, "surely you know Miss Mercer would have let you leave if you had raised your hand?"

"But I did," I cried again, "and she didn't."

The principal turned to my mother. "What am I to do?" She sounded amused, as though children were just odd little creatures who could never be trusted.

My mother looked at her. "Nothing. When it comes to choosing between the word of a teacher and the word of a child I suppose you have to take the teacher's word even if you know the child is telling the truth."

"Really!" Miss Mercer exclaimed.

"It's splendid of you to believe in your little girl so

unreservedly," the principal said, "but in this case I'm sure it was because she was ashamed at having wet her pants that she told you what she did. Isn't that so, Camilla?"

"No," I said.

My mother bowed to the principal and Miss Mercer. "We're arguing in circles. I think I'd better get Camilla home and into dry clothes. And I trust that the next time she asks to be excused she will be excused." And she took me home and gave me a bath and put dry clothes on me and spent all afternoon playing with me, though she was supposed to go somewhere for tea. Then when my father came home they went into his study and talked and talked. And then Father came into my room and took me into the study and sat down and I sat on his lap.

"Camilla," he said, "your mother tells me you had a difficult experience today at school."

"Yes, Father."

"Are you sure you aren't making a mistake when you say that Miss Mercer wouldn't excuse you?"

I knew that I wasn't making a mistake. "Mother believed me!" I cried. "Doesn't she still believe me?"

"She knows you would never tell a lie intentionally," my father said, and I was almost distracted because it seemed to me that now my father and mother believed in Miss Mercer and not in me, and if nobody believed in me, if nobody believed the truth, then something horrible had happened to the truth. But then my father looked at me and said, as though he had suddenly come to a decision, "Your mother believes you and I believe you, and I want you to know that we will never doubt your word under any circumstances whatsoever."

Then I put my head down against him and cried and he rocked me very gently in his arms. Then I asked him. "Father—"

"Yes, Camilla?"

"Miss Mercer told a lie, then."

"Yes, Camilla."

"But she's grown-up."

"Yes."

"I didn't know grown-ups ever told lies."

"Grown-ups aren't so very different from children," he told me. "Some are nice and some aren't. Remember that little girl you met at a party who cheated at all the games?"

"Yes, Father."

"And none of the rest of you liked her because of it?"

"No."

"But you like most of the other children, don't you?"

"Yes, Father."

"Well, it's the same way with adults, darling. Some are very wonderful people and others aren't nice at all. And remember that the principal of your school was in a very difficult position. Only a very fine woman would have realized that she was doing a great wrong in not recognizing the truth; and evidently your principal is not a very fine woman. And another thing to remember, Camilla. Sometimes you can learn a lot from people who really aren't very nice. So don't forget that Miss Mercer still has a lot to teach you about geography—and you've got a lot to learn about it."

I sat there on his lap in silence for a while, then I asked, "Father—you do believe I was telling the truth about asking to be excused?"

"Yes, Camilla. I know you were telling the truth."

I held him very closely then. "Oh, Father," I whispered, "I do love you so."

I sat there on the round bench beside Luisa and stared up at the portrait of three beautiful ladies in white dresses and thought how much I had loved him and I wanted to cry again now as I had cried then; I had to bite my teeth against my lip to keep from crying right there in the museum with people wandering around looking at the pictures.

"What I don't understand," Luisa said, "is why it is necessary for adults to be the way they are. What a stinking business, Camilla. What a stinking lousy thing for an adult to do to a kid. I don't understand how one could."

"No. I don't understand it either." I looked into Luisa's blue eyes, dark with intensity, and I felt very warm toward her because she had not laughed at what I told her, because, though she had not said a great deal, I knew she had understood.

"Listen," she said, "did Frank ever tell you about why he was expelled?"

"Yes." I nodded.

"There you are again. The guy who ran that school ought to have been drawn and quartered. Sure, I think Frank goes overboard about things like that, but when someone you've known the way Frank knew Johnny dies in your arms you oughtn't to be supposed to make sense. I thought Mona'd raise a stink when Frank got kicked out, and she did give him heck, but then she went up and gave the headmaster such a talking to I bet his ear still burns. Listen, Camilla, about Frank."

"What about him?"

"Well—has he ever tried to kiss you or anything?"

I was surprised and I was angry. I was really angry. We had been so close and warm, and now all that warmth was pushed away. "No. Why should he?"

"Frank likes girls and you're pretty. Frank matured very young for a boy. It'd have been much more in character if he'd been kicked out for carrying on with some girl than for religious what-you-may-call-it."

"Whatever made you think of such an idiotic question!" I asked, almost shouting the words at her, and a lady in a mink coat turned around and said, "Girls! Shhh!"

"Well, I thought you might like it if he did kiss you," Luisa said, lowering her voice. "Have you ever been kissed, Camilla?"

"No," I said. I was angrier than I have ever been angry with Luisa.

"Would it surprise you if I said I had? Been kissed, I mean?"

"Not particularly." I was still very angry.

"Well, I have. Even if it seems funny, ugly old Luisa's been kissed."

"It doesn't seem funny."

"Believe me, Camilla," Luisa said, "it's an awful letdown when it happens. It isn't a bit the way it is in the movies. I expected I'd just about swoon but I didn't even particularly like it. Maybe it's because I wasn't in love. It was this slob who took me out one night during last Easter holidays. His mother works on the magazine with Mona and I guess they thought it would be just too cute to get the kids together. He goes to some swanky boarding school and he thought he was a lot smoother than he was. Anyhow, his hair smelled so of brilliantine it almost made me sick. We went to the theater—a stinking musical when I wanted to see an honest-to-goodness play—and all the time he kept holding my hand and his hand was wet and clammy. The only reason I played along with him was for experimental purposes. I mean, a girl who's going to be a doctor ought to know about everything, and I wanted to know what it was really like, going on a date and necking with a boy, if you can call holding hands in the fifth row orchestra necking. Anyhow, he took me out afterward for a sandwich and ginger ale at Sardi's. Then he took me home in a taxi and I'd got to the point where I was so used to subways and buses I'd forgotten what riding in a taxi was like. He held my hand in the taxi and then he kissed me. It was all slobbery and wet and I wiped my mouth on my handkerchief afterward. I guess it hurt his feelings, because he didn't say anything else all the rest of the way home—it was just as we were going by Macy's that he kissed me. But when we got home he came up the steps with me and kissed me again. I was kind of used to it by the second time so I didn't wipe my mouth till after he'd said good-bye and got back in the taxi. Imagine being able to keep a taxi waiting! His father works for one of the big whiskey companies and they always send Mona and Bill a case at Christmas, so I guess he doesn't need to worry. He wrote me a couple of letters when he got back to school, and they were certainly dopey letters. Oh, well. Do you think I should marry for money, Camilla? Should I marry some slob like that? Or should I wait for some nice skinny starving doctor with nice dry lips? If a wet kiss is what that slob gave me, I certainly don't see what's in one. I admit I got my information from Alma Potter. You don't like her, do you?"

"No."

"I think she's kind of a dope too," Luisa said. "She seems to have an awful lot of information, but I bet it isn't all as firsthand as she'd like us to think it is. She said her father was going to give her a mink coat for Christmas this year. I think that's tacky. Oh, golly,

Camilla, I wish I weren't ugly. I wish I could think that slob had kissed me because I was pretty and not just because he kisses every girl he goes out with. I don't believe in marriage, not after what I've seen of it, but I wish I could stay single because I wanted to, and not because I have to." She sat down on a bench in a room full of early Italian church paintings, all reds and blues and golds.

"I bet you're married before I am," I said.

Luisa pushed her fingers viciously through her hair. "It's awful to be ugly, Camilla," she said.

Again I felt sorry for her and fond of her. "Lots of the most famous women in history have been redheads," I said comfortingly, "and none of them got really famous till they were about thirty anyhow."

"Well, maybe I'll improve with maturity. If I decide to be a surgeon it won't make so much difference what I look like. After all, when they operate they're just about all covered up except the eyes. Oh, Camilla, life is so funny, isn't it? Either I'm wildly happy or I'm miserable, and it seems to me most of the time I'm miserable. Never desert me, Camilla. Please, please never desert me."

"Of course I won't desert you," I said, but in a way I knew that I already had. Luisa was my friend, but suddenly she had become my responsibility instead of the other way around. And I knew that this was because of Frank.

Saturday, I thought. I will see Frank on Saturday.

8

Saturday morning I put on my nicest, newest skirt, a full green wool one, and a clean white blouse and a green cardigan. I didn't dare put on my Sunday coat and hat so I just put on my navy blue school coat and my red beret; but instead of just pulling my beret on my head any old how I stood before my mirror for about five minutes trying to get it on the way Michèle Morgan wore hers in a French movie Luisa and I had seen.

Just as I was getting ready to leave, my mother called me into her room. She wore a dress with long sleeves to cover the marks that still showed on her wrists. "Are you going out, darling?" she asked.

"Yes, Mother."

"With whom?"

"Frank Rowan."

"Is Luisa going to be with you?"

"I don't know," I said, and this was the truth. Frank hadn't told me whether or not Luisa was included in his plans, though I doubted it.

My mother frowned for a moment. "Oh, darling, I can't get used to the idea of your having dates. I know it's terrible, but I can't realize I'm old enough to have a daughter who's almost— Sometimes I think I wasn't ever meant to be a mother—I know I haven't been a proper mother to you—but I do love you, my baby, oh, I do, I do."

"I have to go," I said. "I told Frank I'd meet him at ten o'clock."

"I wish I knew whether it's right or not—of course everything's changed nowadays since—but is it all right for you to go out with Frank alone? Do the other girls go out with boys alone?"

"Of course," I said. "Of course it's all right, Mother."

"I ought to talk to Rafferty about it, but I hate to worry him about anything else. When will you be home, darling?"

"I don't know," I said. "Frank said we might have supper with Mr. and Mrs. Stephanowski."

"Who are they?"

"Parents of a friend of his."

"Well—would you telephone me about six o'clock? Then I'll feel easier about you."

"I'll telephone you," I said.

"Promise."

"I promise, Mother."

"And please don't be late, darling, or you'll upset your father. And me too." She pulled me to her and kissed me, saying, "Oh, darling, I love you even if I haven't been a very good— You do know that, don't you? No matter what . . . I'll always love you."

I kissed Mother good-bye and left. Frank was waiting for me on the steps of his house. "Hello, Camilla," he said. He looked at me very seriously, not smiling or holding out his hand in greeting. Then he said, "You look nice," and my heart felt warm and good inside me. He took my arm. "I told David we'd be over this morning. Okay?"

"Yes," I said.

"I didn't tell his mother. She always makes a fuss when David sees anybody new. Says it tires him. My gosh, he's got to have friends. Now is when he needs friends."

We walked over to the apartment on Perry Street where David lived. It had an elevator and we went up to the top floor, the seventh. Frank rang the doorbell and a middle-aged woman in a dark red woolen dress answered it. Her hair was gray and her face was sad; she looked nervous and anxious as she answered the door. Her face fell into long droopy lines; I tried to think what it reminded me of and it was a very old basset hound we had had one summer up in Maine.

"Oh, hello, Frank," she said. "He's not feeling very well today."

"Would you rather we didn't come in, Mrs. Gauss?" Frank asked.

"I don't know. He's always glad to see you, but—" and she looked doubtfully at me.

A voice from inside the apartment called then, "Who is it, Ma?"

"It's Frank and a friend," the woman answered.

"Well, send them in. Don't keep them standing out in the hall."

"Go on in," the woman said.

We followed the sound of the voice into the apartment. Frank went first and I followed him, and because of the apprehensive manner of David's mother, I began now to be frightened. I had never before seen anyone who was maimed in body, and I was afraid that my fear might make me, like Luisa, say the wrong things.

David was sitting in a big armchair. Almost all of his legs had been cut off and a blanket was wrapped around the stumps, which did not reach the edge of the seat of the chair. He had a book in his hand, which he threw down on the table next to him as we entered. In the corner was a folding wheelchair. Frank went over to him and shook his hand and I followed.

"David, this is Camilla Dickinson," Frank said. "She's a friend of mine. I wanted her to meet you. Camilla, this is David Gauss."

David held out his hand to me and I took it. His hand felt very firm and strong and I stood there with his hand over mine, looking down at his face.

He looked older than twenty-seven. Twenty-seven

190

is certainly grown-up, but it ought not to be old, and David seemed old, in spite of a great deal of dark brown hair that looked as though it needed combing. His face was very thin and his eyes seemed to be set too far back in his head. There were deep grooves around his mouth as though he had often to hold his teeth clenched in order to keep from crying out. His nose was thin and delicate and arched like an eagle's.

"So you're a friend of Frank's?" he asked me.

"Yes."

"How did you become friends with him?"

"His sister and I go to school together."

"No reason for being friends. Tell me more than that."

"We talked," I said.

"Better reason. Luisa your friend too?"

"Yes. She's my best friend. I mean—"

"Mean she *was* your best friend?" David asked me, and smiled an odd smile.

Yes, that was exactly what I meant, although it was not until I told David that Luisa was my best friend that I realized it was no longer true.

"Yes," I said, and I looked very hard into David's gray eyes. They were the color of water on a sunless day in winter when the clouds are low and the wind sharp and the water is icy cold, about to freeze.

"In other words," David said, "you like Frank better than Luisa."

"Yes."

"Going to be tough on Luisa, but it's life; sooner or

191

later Luisa's going to have to accept life. Frank, go ask Ma to bring us all in some coffee."

"I'll make it," Frank said, and went out of the room, leaving me alone with David.

But now I wasn't frightened anymore. I did not want to look at the blanket hiding the terrible remains of what had once been two legs as active as Frank's or mine, but as long as I looked at David's face I was not afraid.

"Sit down," David said. "Tell me about yourself. Name again? Camilla what?"

"Camilla Dickinson."

"Call you Miss Dickinson or Camilla?"

"Oh, Camilla," I said. I sat down on a chair just across from David so that I could continue to watch his face. The room we were in was evidently his bedroom, living room, and study combined. There was a hospital bed in one corner covered by a dark red bedspread. There were a lot of books and a big reproduction of a white De Chirico horse and a couple of abstract paintings, very geometrical and with a somehow frightening quality. There was an oriental rug on the floor; and at the windows hung dark red curtains matching the bedspread.

"Are you any relation to Karl Friedrich Gauss?" I asked David.

"The mathematician? No. Not that I know of. Like math?"

"Yes," I said, "and Gauss did the calculations for Piazzi when he discovered the first of the planetoids."

"Mathematician, hunh?" David said. "How old are you?"

"Fifteen. Almost sixteen."

"That's a good age," David said. "First fell in love when I was fifteen. Year behind Stephen Dedalus. Ever read *Portrait of the Artist as a Young Man*?"

"No."

"Ought to. Get Frank to lend it to you. Anyhow, Stephen was fourteen and I was fifteen. Mine was my violin teacher. She was twenty-four. Beautiful as a Siamese cat. Look something like a cat yourself, Camilla, with those big green eyes. Been in love yet, Camilla?"

"No."

"Not in love with Frank?"

When David asked me that it was as though he had taken his clenched fist and hit me with all his power in the stomach. "I hadn't thought about it."

"Why not think about it?" He looked at me with a friendly sort of grin.

"I—I don't know," I stammered, and felt myself blushing. Then I said, "I don't think it's something you have to think about. I think if you're in love you know about it."

"Wise words from one so young," David said, and I could not tell whether or not he was laughing at me. "But sometimes thinking about it does no harm. Get you away from mathematics. Going to be a mathematician like Gauss?"

"I'm going to be an astronomer," I said.

"No kidding?"

"No kidding."

"Math's a good foundation for it." Then, suddenly, David's voice was eager. "Good at cards, by any chance? Like to play cards?"

"Yes. I adore cards."

"Like to come over and play with me sometimes? Frank tries occasionally, like the good kid he is, but he hasn't any card sense; no fun if you win all the time. Papa Stephanowski plays chess with me, but he won't let me lose, either. You play chess?"

"Yes," I said. "I used to. I had a governess once who taught me, and I loved it, but I haven't had any-one to play with since."

"Oh, good, good," David cried, a real light coming into his eyes for the first time. "What a find you are, Camilla. Bless Frank for bringing you over. Camilla, tell me something. I don't frighten you?"

"No," I said.

"Not—repulsive to you?"

"No," I said.

"Sure? Could wear my imitation legs if it bothers you, seeing me like this."

"No," I said.

"Since there's no hope of my ever being able to use real prosthetics and they're just for looks, don't see much point in wearing them. Always depresses me to put them on. Understand that?"

"Yes," I said.

"Bring your chair up closer where I can see you

better," David commanded. "There. That's fine. Don't mind being close to me?"

"No."

"If I could paint I'd like to do your portrait. Why hasn't Frank brought you around before?"

"We've only really known each other for a little while."

"New discovery, hey? Exciting discovering somebody new, isn't it? Camilla, Camilla, glad Frank brought you over this morning. Been—God, been all the way through to China this morning, I've been so low. For some reason you've brought me at least back to limbo again."

Frank came in then with a pot of coffee and some cups on a tray. "I don't make as good coffee as Mrs. Gauss does," he said, "so if it isn't any good you can gripe at me. Dave and I like ours black. How about you, Cam?"

"I'll have it black too." I'd never had coffee black before. Mother doesn't like me to drink coffee and I always have cocoa for breakfast or sometimes tea; the few times I've had coffee it's been with plenty of sugar and cream, or French fashion, with half hot milk. This tasted awful.

"How about some cookies, Frank?" David asked.

"Okay." Frank went back on out. I noticed how long his legs were. They seemed extra long because of David's having no legs. Long and thin and awkward as he walked. I am tall for my age, but Frank is much taller than I am.

"Oh, yes, Camilla," David said as soon as Frank had left the room. "By far the nicest of the girls Frank has brought to see me."

"Has he brought other girls to see you?" I asked. "I mean besides Luisa?"

David looked at me and raised one of his dark, peaked eyebrows. "A few. Very pretty, most of them. But without any importance whatsoever. Glad Frank found you. Better if you were ten years older, but child or not, I'm glad he's found you. Didn't care for that little Italian girl he was going around with. What was her name? Yes. Pompilia Riccioli. No, you're better for Frank than Pompilia, ewe lamb though you are."

I was beginning to hate the name of Pompilia Riccioli. Riccioli of Bologna named most of the craters on the moon, and I wished I could banish Pompilia to one of them.

Frank came in then with the cookies and he and David started talking about the country, about the world. Somehow the things we learn in Current Events at school aren't any closer to me than the things we learn in history. The French Revolution seemed far closer to me than what was going on here or in Europe. But as Frank and David talked it began to become something much nearer to me; it was no longer required reading for school; it was something that had to do with me, personally, Camilla Dickinson. It was something that might affect my entire future life.

I remembered then what Frank and I had talked

about in the park, how to be alive is to be happy. I remembered it because right at this moment I felt more alive than I had ever felt before, and I felt terribly happy.

I wonder why it is so much easier to describe sorrow than it is to describe happiness, even happiness so great that it can make you forget sorrow. I couldn't ever put into words the happiness that I felt whenever I was with Frank, and that I felt that morning talking with Frank and David, even though the things talked about weren't happy. Perhaps it wasn't right to be filled with joy while Frank and David talked about tragic things and with David himself a symbol of these things, but I couldn't help it.

The atmosphere of the room, though they were talking about death and destruction, seemed to me to be full of life and construction. These were the kind of people who belonged to life, to the kind of world I wanted to grow up into; and it was people like my mother who did not like to talk about the war or the future or anything unpleasant who belonged to death and the past. I must have looked very solemn thinking these things because Frank broke out of a long speech and said, "I'm sorry if we're distressing you, Camilla, but I think when you come to the end of a civilization you ought to be aware of it."

But sitting there, listening to Frank and David, civilization seemed for me not to be ending, but to be beginning.

And now the amazing thing was that while they

were talking about the war, and about hate and evil and love and life, I suddenly stopped hating my mother. It wasn't that I felt about her the way I used to, the old secure uncomplicated way; but now I no longer resented her being Rose Dickinson. Sitting there and being excited because I was Camilla Dickinson and alive, I knew suddenly that I would be able to put my arms around my mother and kiss her good night again with love. I could love her in spite of Jacques. Then I tried not to hate Jacques, but the best I could do was to make my mind a gray blank about him. I turned my mind back to Frank and David and the things they were talking about, and I asked David, "Is there going to be another world war?" And I forgot my mother and Jacques and began to shiver inside myself.

David looked at me and there was dark rage in his eyes. "What do you think?"

"I—I don't know." I held myself very still in my chair because I didn't want either David or Frank to see my fear.

David looked at me for a long moment and his mouth was very tight with pain, but I could not tell whether it was his body that was paining him, or his heart. "Always another war," he said. "Always has been, always will be. Frank will go off to it and he'll come back looking like me, or he'll come back blind, or without hands, or arms. Or not at all. Or perhaps I am being optimistic. Maybe there won't be anything to come back to. Just a gaping hole in the universe to show where our particular brand of fools lived and committed suicide. I shock you, Camilla? I make you unhappy? Can't help it. You're old enough to realize these things."

"Yes," I said.

"No man can participate in mass murder and not lose his understanding of the value of human life. But it has a value, Camilla. Even a life like mine. Life is the greatest gift that could ever be conceived, but before any of us ever were born those who had gone before us had already deprived it of half its value. A daffodil pushing up through the dark earth to the spring, knowing somehow deep in its roots that spring and light and sunshine will come, has more courage and more knowledge of the value of life than any human being I've met. Model yourself after the daffodil, Camilla. Have the courage to push your head up out of the darkness."

Frank said with a grin, "I told Camilla her education had been neglected. You're making up for it even faster than I'd expected, Dave."

"Too much for you, Camilla?" David asked.

"No," I said, and this was true. I was frightened, but I felt also a tremendous grateful awe that they should be talking to me in this way, that they should be taking the trouble to try to educate me. David had said that all the other girls Frank had brought to see him were completely unimportant. Did that mean that he thought that I was not unimportant?

"After the last war," David was saying, "I mean the one before mine, there was the lost generation. Difference was that then everybody was so conscious of being lost. They *wanted* to be lost. Enjoyed it. Weren't really afraid. Still had a future. We're the ones who're really lost. Don't mean me, or anybody else who was personally ruined by the war, but all the kids today. You, Camilla. Frank. You don't want to be lost."

"No," Frank said.

David held out his empty cup. "Pour me another cup of coffee." And as he took a sip out of his fresh cup and put it back on the table he said, "Do you suppose God feels about his creation—world and its people—the way a writer feels about his work? Same joy of inspiration, and then the horrible depression when it goes wrong, when it loses its nobility of conception? Wouldn't blame him for ripping this one out of the typewriter and stuffing it into the incinerator." Then he looked sharply at me. "Nothing to say, Camilla?"

I shook my head.

"Very rare quality in a woman," he said, "the ability to keep quiet when you have nothing to say. Is she always like that, Frank? Or is it just my influence?"

"She's always like that," Frank said.

Suddenly a strange look came to David's eyes, as though he were moving far, far away from us. His eyes seemed to go back and back, and the lines cut in his face seemed all at once to grow deeper. He reached for a small box on the table by him and took out a pill. Frank got up quickly and poured him a glass of water from a pitcher that stood on the table and as

200

David reached for it I could see that his hand was shaking. He swallowed the pill and drank some water and leaned his head back against the chair, his lids drawn tightly over his eyes. Frank waited until at last the eyes were open again, and then said, "We'd better go now, Dave."

David smiled, but it was a difficult smile; it was as though it took a great deal of muscular power for him to pull the corners of his mouth upward; and the smile scarcely came into his eyes at all. "Okay," he said. Then he looked at me and said slowly, with difficulty, "When will you come play . . . chess with me, Camilla? Can you . . . come tomorrow? It's Sunday."

I was going to a concert with my mother in the afternoon, so I said, "I could come tomorrow evening after supper."

"All right," David said. "Thank you." He closed his eyes again and his voice, too, seemed to go off into the distance. Frank and I left him. As we passed what I guess must have been the living room, Frank called out good-bye to Mrs. Gauss, who had the radio turned on very low to some woman's program as she sat there sewing. It was an odd sort of room to me, like the living rooms in some of the foreign films Luisa and I had been to, dusty and dark in color, with a round table covered by a long brown velvet throw, and a hanging lamp over it with fringe on the shade.

Mrs. Gauss came to the door with us. "Good-bye, Frank. It's good of you to come so often."

"I like coming," Frank said. "This is Camilla Dickinson. I don't think I introduced you when we came in."

Mrs. Gauss and I both murmured how-do-you-do and good-bye and Frank and I left. We went down the elevator in silence and we walked slowly along the street and then Frank said, "You don't mind going back tomorrow night?"

"No."

"Did you like David?"

"Yes. I—"

"What?"

"Oh, Frank," I said, "it's the first time I—oh, I knew there was a war and everything, I even saw about it in the newsreels, I was scared of it, but none of it—I didn't know. I didn't realize. Frank, I don't think most people do."

When I was first getting to know Luisa I felt that she was giving me glimpses of worlds I'd never seen, almost as though she were giving me a telescope to look through at the stars; but I realized now that Frank's telescope was much stronger than Luisa's; or perhaps it was only that it was more suited to my eyes.

"Hungry?" Frank asked me then. "Ready for lunch?"

"Yes," I said. "I think I am."

"The paper says it's going to snow tonight."

"Good. I hope it does," I said. "I love snow." And I thought how wonderful it would be to walk about the streets in the snow with Frank, to feel the snow feather-soft on our faces and hands, and to walk along the quiet streets that somehow seem so much narrower, so much more intimate, during a snowfall.

We ate spaghetti in a small Italian restaurant that Frank said was owned by the parents of a friend of his, and all the time we ate we talked, talked, talked. It seemed as though if we talked forever we would never finish saying all the things we had to say to each other. After lunch we walked. We weren't walking anywhere in particular, just wandering slowly along the streets and talking, and the sky was gray and full and heavy, and one or two flakes of snow drifted gently down.

"It's starting to snow," Frank said.

"Yes."

"David doesn't ask many people to come see him. There are one or two people who come quite often, but not many. And he doesn't like strangers. I'm glad he liked you."

"I am too," I said.

Frank pulled his hand out of the pocket of his overcoat and took my hand. When he had taken my hand once in the park, other times when I had touched his fingers, it had seemed quite natural and unimportant. Now I was terribly conscious in each finger, in my palm, in every bit of the skin of my hand, of the contact between us. I could feel it somehow not just in my hand but all over me. It was such a big feeling, such a strange one, that we walked for quite a while and I hardly heard anything that Frank was saying because the feel of his hand seemed to fill my ears too.

Then I heard him still talking about David. "You know, Cam, I've always been terribly—proud—somehow, that David has cared enough about me to want me to come see him. I mean he—I mean, I must seem just a kid to him, and he really talks to me as though I were—" Then he broke off and looked at me and said, "Gee, Camilla, you look pretty today! That color you have on. I was noticing it at lunch. It sort of goes with your eyes. . . . There's a good movie on at the Eighth Street. Let's go, hunh?"

We sat together in the darkness at the movies and it was a good picture, but I was too conscious of Frank sitting there beside me really to keep my mind on it. Afterward I remembered I'd promised to call Mother, so we went to a phone booth and I called my mother to tell her I was all right, and for a moment I was no longer all right because the line was busy and I was afraid she might be talking with Jacques. But when the line was cleared and I talked to her, her voice was clear and casual and I went back out to Frank and forgot about her and was with Frank, all of me. It's a funny thing how sometimes your body can be in a room with people, but you yourself won't really be there; you'll be with someone else who isn't in the room at all. But all of me was with Frank and I kept thinking, I wonder if I will ever be as happy as this again.

Then we just walked very quietly for a while, holding hands, and all about us the first real snow of the winter started to fall, dropping its soft white stars between the houses onto the street, falling so softly, so tenderly about us. All the city noises seemed muted, muffled in whiteness. The streetlamps came on, the light streaming from them in moving gold arcs. The intimacy of streets is more beautiful and comforting when it is snowing than at any other time. The snow curls around the corners, falls like silence between the houses, piles over the curb so that street and sidewalk are lost in white. I knew that by tomorrow the snowplows would have cleaned the streets, feet would have smutched the sidewalks, the remaining snow would be black and soiled; but as I walked through the evening, holding Frank's hand, the snow was free and pure, and it seemed part of my happiness.

We went to the Stephanowskis for supper and they made me feel warm and welcome. After supper we played some new recordings Mr. Stephanowski had brought over from the shop, and then it was time to go home. I didn't dare stay out too late.

Frank said, "Camilla, I wish I could take you home in a taxi, but I'm afraid it will have to be the subway."

"I'd rather go in the subway anyhow," I said.

The snow had stopped falling, though the sky was still full of snow clouds. With the snow on the ground and the heavy white clouds hanging low over the city, everything seemed touched by a strange white light, almost the way you might expect it to look on the moon.

When we got out of the subway and started walking toward the apartment house, Frank and I were suddenly very quiet, as though the talking we had been doing all day had drained us of words. I felt that I could not say another thing because now the beautiful long day was over and I knew that it had been the biggest day of my life so far. I thought that I could not bear it because the day was over and I did not know when I would see Frank again. He had said nothing and I could not ask.

Then, suddenly, in the middle of the quiet snowy street, Frank stopped and said, "Camilla."

We stood there very still in the street and we were alone; there was no one coming in either direction; there were only dark houses on either side and the snow between. We stood there very close together, and almost without moving we seemed to become closer and Frank's cold clean cheek was pressed against mine. We stood there with our cheeks together, cold and clean, and I felt my heart beating terribly rapidly, and I could hear Frank's, too, a strong swift thumping against my chest.

Then without saying anything we started walking again. We walked until we got to the house and then Frank just said, "Good-bye, Camilla," in an odd sort of way and left me.

The elevator boy leered at me and said, "Haven't seen your boyfriend lately."

"What?"

"Your boyfriend. Mr. Nissen." He gave a strangling sort of giggle.

"Oh, him," I said, and it was as though I hadn't heard because my mind never touched even the thought of Jacques. I was still out in the snow with Frank and I thought I would die of agony because he had left me without saying anything about seeing me again.

When the door of the elevator had closed behind me I stood in the hall without pulling out my latchkey and things I had not noticed during the day came back to me: David's saying that I was the nicest of the girls Frank had brought to see him. Who were the other girls? What about Pompilia Riccioli? Luisa had said that Frank liked girls. Perhaps I was just one of dozens of girls Frank liked for a day and then dropped in favor of someone else.

But then I thought, No. I couldn't have been as happy as I was all day if it hadn't meant something to Frank too.

That night I dreamed a dream. I dreamed that I was standing on a cold and snowy plateau somewhere at the isolated edges of the world. I was standing there all alone, and all about me the snow was falling. No matter in which direction I turned I could see nothing but snow. Snow on the ground, snow in the sky, snow falling in the air about me. And I knew that I was terribly frightened and terribly alone. Then, out of nowhere, Frank was standing beside me. He said, "Camilla," the way he had said it on the snowy sidewalk, and then he took me and held me tightly in his arms and kissed me. When he kissed me in this dream all the snow melted away and we were standing in a green field filled with flowers, with tulips and narcissi and daffodils and irises, with all the flowers that had had the courage to push up through the snow, knowing that spring would be there.

Then I woke up. I didn't know what time it was, but it couldn't have been terribly late, because there were still lights on across the court. And suddenly, for no reason that I could explain, I flung around on my pillow and began to sob. I sobbed and sobbed and I couldn't stop and I was terribly afraid that Mother or Father would hear. I pressed my face into the pillow and finally the sobs stopped coming. But there remained an awful aching in my body and all I wanted in the world was to be standing out on the snowy street again, close to Frank, with my cheek against his.

Then I thought about his kissing me in the dream, and I tried to imagine what it would be like if he really kissed me, and I knew that I wanted him to kiss me more than anything in the world.

The next morning at first I didn't remember the dream. I got up and took off my pajamas and stood in front of the long mirror on my door looking at myself almost in the same way I had looked at myself on that morning of my birthday when I had first realized I was Camilla Dickinson. I stood there naked and looking at myself until I began to shiver, and then I dressed and went into Mother's room; and I was able to put my arms around her as she lay in bed waiting for her breakfast tray, and kiss her, and say, "Good morning, Mother."

Her arms went around me terribly quickly, terribly gladly, and she said, "Oh, good morning, my darling, my darling, good morning."

My father was standing in front of his mirror tying his tie, and I said, "Good morning, Father."

He smiled at me. "We seem to have our old Camilla back."

Oh, no, I wanted to tell him. This is a new Camilla, an entirely different Camilla.

But I just said, "Well, I think I'll go call Luisa."

"Oh?" my father said. "Does that mean Luisa or her brother?"

"It means Luisa," I said. "I thought maybe I'd go down to see her this morning."

"I see," my father said. "Well, I'm delighted that you've decided to consult us about it this time, at any rate."

"Don't, Raff," my mother said quickly. "Don't take your bad mood out on Camilla."

"Are you in a bad mood, Father?" I asked.

"Your mother says I am."

"Camilla darling, I'm so glad you enjoyed—" my

mother said. "Frank must be a nice boy to have given you such a happy day yesterday."

"Yes." I thought of the day and I was excited and happy. And I was frightened because I was afraid there might never be another like it.

"I don't like your being out alone so late at night," my father said.

"I wasn't alone. I was with Frank."

"Frank's just a child."

"Frank is seventeen," I said. "Next year he's going to college."

"Oh, let her enjoy herself these last few weeks, Rafferty," my mother said.

My father gave a start of annoyance. I was suddenly very frightened. "What did you mean, 'these last few weeks'?" I asked.

"Camilla, oh, darling," my mother said, "your father and I have—I'm sure it's the best thing for you, the very best—we've talked and talked about it."

"About what?" I asked.

My father turned around and looked at me. "Camilla, I'm going out now. I wish there were time for us to have a talk before I go but there isn't. I'll have to talk to you when I get back."

"I want to know what it is now!" I cried, and there was panic in my heart.

"I haven't time to talk to you now, dear," my father said. "I'll be back for supper and I'll talk to you then."

"I'm going out right after supper," I said. "Please, Father, what is it?"

"Who are you going out with after supper?" my father asked. "Luisa? Or Frank?"

"I'm going to see David," I said. "David Gauss. I promised I'd play chess with him."

"Camilla, really," my father said. "You pick the most inconvenient times— Who on earth is David Gauss? Where did you meet him and why are you playing chess with him?"

"Raff, go on." Mother sat up in bed and frowned anxiously. "I'll talk to Camilla."

"I intend to wait long enough to learn who David Gauss is," Father said.

"He's a veteran," I cried. "He lost both his legs in the war. Frank took me to see him yesterday. He can't ever walk again and he has no one to play chess with and I know how to play."

"Oh," Father said, and he sounded less irritable and excited. "I see. Where does he live?"

"On Perry Street."

"In the Village?"

"Yes."

"He certainly doesn't expect you to go all the way down to Perry Street alone and back at night, does he?" Father asked.

I began to feel angry. "I don't think he thought about it. He doesn't know where I live."

"I'm sorry, Camilla," Father said, "but I can't allow you to make that trip alone at night."

"I've been to Luisa's alone."

"Not with my knowledge."

"I have to go," I said. "I promised."

"I'm sorry, Camilla," Father said again. "I forbid you to go there alone, and that's final."

"Perhaps Carter could take her down," Mother suggested.

"Carter goes off on Sunday evening."

"Father," I said, "David was in the war. He lost both his legs. I promised him. I have to keep my promise."

My father opened his mouth to speak again and the telephone rang. Mother answered it. "Hello? . . ." She held the receiver out to me. "It's for you, darling. I think it's Frank."

It was. "Hi, Cam," he said. "Listen, about your going to see David tonight. Do you want me to take you?"

It was as though somehow he had heard the conversation between me and my parents and was coming to my rescue. "Oh, Frank, that would be wonderful!" I cried.

"Well, listen," he said, "if it's okay with your mother I'll pick you up at Carnegie after your concert and we'll go out and get something to eat and then I'll take you over to David's and bring you home."

"Oh, Frank, that would be wonderful," I said again. "Wait a minute and I'll ask Father." I turned to my father. "Father," I said, "Frank says he'll take me to David's and bring me home."

"Will he call for you here?" Father asked.

"He wants me to have supper with him," I said. "He'll pick me up at Carnegie after the concert and then he'll take me to David's and bring me home."

"Very well, dear," Father said. "This one time."

"It's all right," I said to Frank. "He says it's all right." And I felt as though a whole sky full of birds had risen up inside me and were flying to the sun.

My father pulled me to him roughly. "I'm sorry if I've seemed disagreeable this morning. I'm trying to get a million and one things done in a short time and it makes me irritable. I'll be off now." He patted me on the shoulder and then turned to Mother and said, "I'm sorry, Rose. I've been a bear this morning. Forgive me."

My mother put her arms around my father then and clung to him. The strange thing was that never before had I seen my mother do anything that I felt to be *me*, but now she clung to my father in the way in which I would have liked to cling to Frank. I moved over to the window because I felt that perhaps I shouldn't be looking.

My father stood there for a moment, holding my mother. Then he said, "All right, Rose. Relax. Calm down."

I turned and saw my mother's face and she looked as though my father had struck her. She said, "Oh, Raff—"

And my father said, "Okay, say it. Get it off your chest."

My mother said, "I've tried to say it so many times, and it never seems to mean anything to you."

I could see that my father was trying to be patient. "You've been trying to say what?"

213

"And I can't say it now. I can't say what I want to say. I hold you—I—I clutch you, because I love you so desperately, and time is so short, we have such a little time in which to live and be young, even at best, and I put my arms around you and hold you because I want to love you while I can and I want to *know* I'm loving you, only it doesn't mean anything because you aren't afraid. You aren't frightened so that you want to clutch it all while you can."

Now I knew that they had forgotten that I was in the room, standing half obscured by the window draperies, and I was afraid to move, because I felt that this was very big, that what my mother was trying to tell my father was terribly important, and if I moved, even the smallest bit to let them remember I was there, it might break it.

My mother said, "Jacques is afraid. That's why—"

"Why what?" my father asked harshly.

"We hold each other because we're afraid and there's so little time for love and comfort."

Now my father's voice was rough. "You can say that in almost the same breath that you say you love me!"

My mother gave a cry of despair. "You see, you see! I've tried to tell you again and you don't understand!"

My father turned and left the room and all of a sudden I realized that he was crying. I had seen my mother cry so many times I couldn't count them and it always distressed me, but it didn't rock my founda-

214

tions. If my father cried then Atlas's foot indeed had slipped.

My mother stood very still for a moment. Then she rushed out after my father. I waited by the window for a long time, my cheek pressed against the cold glass, but they did not come back.

9

That afternoon before the concert I asked my mother, "What is it Father was going to tell me?"

"He wants to tell you himself, darling," my mother said.

"But I'm not going to be home this evening when he comes back so couldn't you tell me now?"

"Oh, no, darling, no, I can't possibly. I shouldn't have said anything about it this morning. Anyhow it's —it's really nothing to get upset about." And she started talking about getting me some new clothes.

They played the Prokofiev Third Piano Concerto that afternoon and I tried to pretend that Frank was sitting beside me instead of Mother, and I wondered if perhaps Mother would let Frank go with me some Sunday. Then the music caught me up and I was lost in it and somehow while I was listening, there was

216

again the strange feeling as though I were part of a dream. This was the music Frank had chosen for my music and now it seemed to me that it was our music, because if it made Frank think of me, to me it *was* Frank.

"Enjoying yourself, darling?" Mother whispered.

"Yes."

Frank was waiting for us after the concert. "Mother," I said, "this is Frank Rowan. Frank, this is my mother."

It was all they could do in the mob on the steps to shake hands. Frank said, "I'll take care of her, Mrs. Dickinson, and I'll try not to keep her out too late," and I could tell by my mother's smile that she liked him.

Then we were alone and Frank said, "We'd better eat right away, Camilla. I promised David I'd bring you over early." Then he looked at me in my dark green Sunday coat and hat. "Camilla, you look so pretty today. It seems to me every day you look prettier."

We went downtown to the same restaurant we had had lunch at the day before. Most of the snow was gone from the streets; the sad remnants lay in soiled piles near the curbs. Now that it was evening it had turned colder and what had been slush when Mother and I went to the concert was slippery ice.

As we sat down in the restaurant Frank said, "Mona and Bill had another fight this afternoon. It gets so I hate to be home. I wish I could go away to college next year, but with dough the way it is it'll probably be NYU. Not that I have anything against NYU. I just wish I could go someplace where I didn't have to live at home."

The proprietor of the restaurant, who had not been there the day before, came over to us and said, "Good evening, Franky boy," and Frank said, "Evening, Mr. Riccioli. How's everything at your house?"

When I heard the name Riccioli I felt icy cold. I sat terribly still as Mr. Riccioli said, "Fine, fine," rubbing his hands together. "Pompilia, she's asking why you don't come around no more."

"I've been busy with school," Frank said. "Tell her I'll come see her soon."

Mr. Riccioli looked with perfectly friendly interest at me. "You got a new girl friend?"

"Sure," Frank said. "You know me. I get a new girl friend every week. But Pompilia's still the queen of them all."

"Good, good," Mr. Riccioli said. "My Pompilia, she's a beautiful girl. She's got lots of boyfriends. It's nice for a girl to have lots of boyfriends."

Some other people came in then, and he went off to talk to them. I looked down at my plate.

"I was nuts to come here," Frank said, "but the old man usually isn't around on weekends, and it's as cheap as any place I know." He sounded angry.

"Oh."

"Listen, that didn't mean anything, what I said about new girl friends. I mean, I had to say it so the old man

218

wouldn't think I was ditching his daughter. I've never felt about anybody the way I feel about you, Camilla. The others—well, I only liked their looks, their outsides. With you I like both your outsides and your insides. Pompilia and I just had a good time together. Fun. She doesn't give any more of a hang for me than I do for her. I wouldn't have come here otherwise. I haven't seen Pompilia to talk to for a couple of months. Listen, how about having ravioli tonight? Or would you rather have a pizza?"

"Ravioli, I guess," I said. Then, "Luisa said last Saturday you were having lunch with Pompilia Riccioli," and I knew right away that I had been idiotically stupid, that I had made Frank angry.

"So?" he said. "Not that it's anybody's business, but I had lunch with David."

"I didn't mean—" I started, and then finished lamely, "I'm sorry, Frank."

"Forget it," Frank said. "Luisa just—oh, forget it. Tell me something about stars. I like to hear you talk about stars. What's the difference between a star and a planet? How do you tell them apart?"

"The easiest way is that a star twinkles and a planet doesn't."

"Go on," Frank said. "Tell me about planets."

"Well—Mercury is closest to the sun, then Venus, Earth, Mars, Jupiter, Saturn, Uranus, Neptune, Pluto. Kepler thought there ought to be a planet between Mars and Jupiter, because the space between them is so much bigger than the space between any of the other planets, and that's how Piazzi found the first planetoid, looking for a planet."

Frank said, "Tell me something about Saturn. Isn't that the one with the ring?"

"Yes," I said. "The ring casts a big shadow. That's why you can see it so easily, but it's really about as thin as a piece of paper. Another sort of interesting thing about Saturn is that sometimes, if you're in a place where stars are clear, it casts a real shadow that you can see."

"I never thought of stars as having shadows," Frank said. "I wonder if anybody's written a poem or anything about that? You really do know a lot about it."

I shook my head. "No, I don't. I don't know anything at all. Anybody could know the things I know. It doesn't even begin to make me an astronomer. I'll have to study all kinds of higher mathematics. I mean the algebra and geometry we get at school aren't really anything."

"This summer," Frank said, "we'll have to get out in the country together somehow and look at the stars."

And I thought, If Frank is planning about the summer I can't be just another Pompilia Riccioli.

As soon as we had finished eating, Frank took me over to Perry Street. "I have to go back home and do some studying, Cam," he said. "You give me a buzz when you're ready to go home and I'll come right over for you. It won't take me more than five minutes to walk back."

"All right," I said.

Frank said good evening to Mrs. Gauss and then he left, saying, "I'll come in and say hello to Dave when I come back for Camilla."

Mrs. Gauss took me into the living room. The light over the round table was warm and red in the center of the room and then went off into dark mysterious shadows in the corners. The heavy furniture seemed to repel the light and a feeling of rejection and disapproval loomed at me from the shadows. I stood by the table and Mrs. Gauss stood in the shadows looking at me. She did not say anything; she just kept on staring at me as though she were trying to find out something from my face. Then at last she said, "You'd better not stay too long, Miss Dickinson. He's had one of his bad days. I wanted to call and tell you not to come but he insisted on seeing you." There was another pause. Then she said, "Please don't think I don't appreciate your coming. I'm very grateful to you. There are so few people he's willing to see. I get frantic because he just sits and broods and refuses to see his old friends who want to come cheer him up."

Then she said, "I had three sons once. David is all I have left." She stared at me for a long moment as though she hated me. Then she said, "He's waiting. Go on in to him."

I fled from the lamplit center of the room, across the edge of shadow, down the hall, and into David's room.

He was lying in the hospital bed. The bed was raised and he was propped up against pillows. I looked at his face; I did not look where the blankets flattened out suddenly, where his legs ended. He held out his hand. "Come in, Camilla." He smiled at me and the smile sent an ache into my stomach.

I went over to the bed and took his hand. I stood there looking at his face and he took both his hands and held mine. "Those eyes of yours, Camilla," he said. "Solemn. Penetrating. What do you see when you stare at a body like that?"

I saw only that he was terribly tired, that he was still in pain. That was something anybody could have seen. It was *his* eyes, I felt, that were able to look deep into me and understand things about me that I didn't understand myself.

"Thanks for coming," he said. "Sure you don't mind?"

"No. I wanted to come."

"My sake or yours?"

"For mine." This was true. When I looked at David's face I felt that behind the lines of pain and suffering was a knowledge of all the answers, and that perhaps if I talked to him enough, or even looked at him enough, he might be able to give me some of the answers.

"Okay, then," he said. "Forgive me for receiving you in bed. Had a bad day. This is less tiring than the chair. If my mother talked any rubbish about not staying too long, please ignore it. I'll tell you when I want you to go." He still held his hands about mine. Then he said,

"Camilla, since I'm in bed this evening, been wondering about the best way to have our game. Thought, if it doesn't bother you, if you don't mind too much, you could push the hospital table across the bed, up close to me; then you could sit on the foot of the bed. I don't have any legs for you to get tangled in. Would that— Is that okay with you?"

"Yes," I said. I drew my hand out of his and pushed the hospital table up from the foot of the bed until it was in a position where he could reach it easily.

"Cards and chess set are in the bottom drawer of my desk," he said.

I got them and then I climbed up onto the foot of his bed and sat, cross-legged, opposite him. We started off with double solitaire. He taught me some new games, and I showed him a couple he hadn't known. He was wonderful to play with. Usually when I play cards with Luisa or any of the kids at school it's much too easy to win and they think so slowly that I get bored with the game. This year some of them have started giving what they call bridge parties; mostly they don't play cards; they just sit and talk about the other kids who aren't at the party, and then they have something gooey to eat. But David's mind clicked sharp and clean. I forgot that I was sitting on the hospital bed just about where his knees ought to have been, and thought only of the game.

After a while he said, "Talk for a while and give me a chance to rest; then we'll try chess."

"All right."

"Look," he said, "would you pour me a glass of water and give me one of those pills from that box? Thanks, honey. Know you're a good kid, Camilla? Very good kid." He looked at me and smiled. "Got to the point now where I just can't be bothered with people who don't interest me. Try to bother with them, I get exhausted. You interest me very much, know that? Feel you're in the middle of a period of change, growth. All at once things that have been lying dormant in you are unfolding. Like that daffodil pushing up to spring. Right, Camilla? Suddenly waking up, aren't you?"

"I don't know," I said. "I certainly don't feel like a daffodil. And if what I'm feeling is waking up, then it's a terribly confusing thing to wake up."

"Don't you think the daffodil's confused, hunh? Sky and sun must seem terrifying after the dark security of being buried in the earth."

"I wonder why they come up, then," I said.

"Frank's right. Life is more valuable than death. Jung says there's no coming to life without pain. True for you, isn't it, Camilla?"

"Yes," I said.

"Like to go back to the old security if you could?"

"Yes," I said.

"Why?"

"I don't—" I started, stumbling over my words. "It's too— I don't think I'm ready to grow up."

"You are, Camilla," David said. "Nobody ever thinks he's ready. Most people don't think about it at all one way or other. Very fact you're thinking about it proves you're ready."

"I still think I'd rather be secure," I said.

David laughed and reached for my hand again. "First place," he told me, "no such thing as security. Doesn't exist. Only a feeling of security."

"Then I'd like to have that feeling."

"No, Camilla. Not really. If you were secure, things wouldn't change, would they?"

"I guess not."

"Without change, uncertainty, fear that goes with them, we wouldn't *be*."

"What do you mean? Why not?"

David held my hand tightly. "In order to be, honey, we must progress. Once we stop moving we die. In order to progress we must change. Part of growing up. Suppose it's natural for you to have your old childish wish for security, but the only complete security is death."

"No!"

"Yes," David said. "Yes. Even if we fear it, as Frank does, as the complete insecurity. But somewhere in infinity opposites meet, hunh? Look at it with eyes open, life is the greatest of all arguments for insecurity. Hunh, darling?"

How different the word "darling" was when David used it from the way it was when Mother used it and from the way it was when Jacques used it. With David it was something warm and tender and in some way a little frightening.

"Okay," David said. "Let's have that game of chess. Set up the board, will you?"

When we started to play I realized that I had forgotten a good deal, but as we played, it came back to me, though David beat me quickly and rather badly.

But he said, "It's okay, Camilla. Couldn't sit back and win with my eyes closed the way I usually do. Play with me a few more times and we'll be having real games. Try another?"

"Yes," I said.

But we had not finished setting up the board when Mrs. Gauss came to the doorway. "David, it's time for you to get ready for bed."

"Oh, Ma," David said in a tired voice, "what earthly difference does it make when I go to bed? Where am I except in bed anyhow?"

"You know what happens when you get overtired—especially when you've had such a bad day."

"What time is it, please?" I asked.

"After nine."

"Oh!" I cried. "Then I do have to get home. I'm supposed to be in bed early except Friday and Saturday." I got down off David's hospital bed and stood beside it.

"Okay," David said. "Call Frank, Ma. Tell him Camilla's ready. And for God's sake don't worry about me. Haven't had such a good evening in weeks.

Now Camilla and I'll talk until Frank comes for her. Then I'll brush my teeth for you, meek as a lamb."

Mrs. Gauss smiled back at him then, a smile that was twisted and difficult, and left us.

As she closed the door behind her David said, "Come again, Camilla?"

"Yes," I said. "Of course."

"When?"

"I could come some afternoon after school. Or any time during the weekend. I'm not supposed to go out weekday evenings."

"Come because you want to? Or because you pity me and think you ought to? Don't lie."

"Because I want to."

"Pity me?"

"Yes," I said.

He reached out and took my hand and pulled me a little closer to the bed. "Honest with me. Thanks, honey. Of course you pity me. But on the other rare occasions when I've asked the question there's been a lot of stalling. Hate pity, Camilla. If I could dispense with the pity of my so-called fellow human beings I could stand this whole damn mess better. Horrible to my mother. Make her angry to drive the pity out of her. Think you and Frank pity me less, or differently, than anybody else I know. Know you're going to be a very beautiful woman, Camilla?"

"People have told me that this past year," I said.

"Know it yourself?"

"I don't quite know," I told him. "I look at myself

227

in the mirror and try to see it, but I can't see anything but just the Camilla Dickinson I've been looking at all my life. It's when I'm not near a mirror and can't see myself or really remember how I look—because I can't remember how I look when I'm not directly facing a mirror—that I feel beautiful. I feel beautiful when I'm with Frank."

"Feel beautiful when you're with me?"

"Yes," I said.

Then David smiled at me and for some reason I wanted to cry. I even felt tears rushing to my eyes, and I pushed, pushed them back.

"Sweet, Camilla. You're sweet," David said, and he reached out with his hand and stroked my hair. As he touched my hair with his gentle strong hand a soft warmth seemed to go all through my body.

"Oh, Camilla," David said. "Camilla."

I stood there close beside the bed and again he lifted his hand and ran it over my hair, and again that strange sweet warmth flowed over me. "Camilla," David said, "I could teach you so much, if—" He broke off abruptly, picked up one of the chess men and looked at it, and then placed it back on the board. "Isn't time for any more chess. How about a quick game of that double solitaire you showed me?"

We played and again it was exciting for me to see how much quicker, how much clearer his mind was than mine. I had the cards though, and I won. He pushed the cards aside then, and smiled at me.

"You're a joy, Camilla. A great joy. Do something for me?"

"What?"

"Kiss me good night?"

"Yes."

"Don't object to kissing someone like me?"

"No. Why should I?" I said. It was only when David mentioned his legs that I became aware that he was different from other men, that he had to keep reassuring himself that I wasn't frightened by him, or repelled. I wondered if other people had been repelled; and I knew that he would always know.

He drew me to him, very gently, very firmly, and then he kissed me. I had expected him to kiss me on the forehead or on the cheek; but he put his lips against mine, lightly, at first, and then with increasing pressure. Again the soft warmth flowed over and through my body. It wasn't until he took his lips away that I thought suddenly, I have been kissed. This is my first kiss. And Frank didn't give it to me.

"My sweet, pure, untouched little Camilla," David said. "My unborn, untarnished, unawakened little Camilla. How I wish I—" Then he took my hands and held them so tightly that I couldn't help gasping. He released them immediately. "Sorry, darling," he said. "Wouldn't hurt you for anything in the world."

We heard Frank in the hall then and I moved away from the bed and picked up my coat and hat.

"Hi, Cam; hi, Dave," Frank said as he came in and

went over to David to shake his hand. "Who trounced who—or whom trounced whom?"

"No one trounced nobody," David said. "Camilla's a most exciting partner."

"Ready, Cam?" Frank asked.

"Yes." I went over to David's bed again and looked at him. I looked at his face, at his eyes that were dark with suffering and yet alive with what I felt to be the wisdom of the ages; and I looked at his lips, pulled tight with pain and at the same time full of tenderness, and I thought, David kissed me, and Frank has not kissed me, except in a dream.

"Next weekend, Camilla?" David asked me.

"Yes," I said. "Next weekend."

Frank and I said good night to Mrs. Gauss and then we walked over to the subway. Frank talked but somehow I couldn't say anything. All that came to my lips to say was, Frank, David kissed me, and I knew I could not say that.

After a while Frank asked me, "Camilla, are you all right?"

"Yes."

"You seem so sort of brooding. . . . David didn't upset you about anything or anything?"

"No," I said.

"Okay. I just didn't want anything to be worrying you. You go ahead and be silent if you want to."

We walked along in silence and I was grateful because I knew Frank wouldn't ask me any more questions. Anytime Luisa thought I had anything on my mind she would be at me and at me, trying to find out what it was; but I knew that Frank would leave me alone.

When we left the subway I remembered walking home the night before, and how we had stopped in the newly fallen snow and stood close together, our cheeks touching. And I knew suddenly that that had been much more important than David's kiss.

We reached the place where we had stopped but there was someone walking down the street toward us and the snow had all melted and the sidewalk was bare and Frank did not stop and I didn't know whether or not he even remembered.

As we neared our apartment house someone came out of the door, called good night to the doorman, and walked swiftly toward us. It was Jacques.

I stopped very still and Frank said, "What's the matter?"

"I can't go home," I said. "I can't go home."

"What is it, Cam?" Frank asked me, and his face in the light of the streetlamp was furrowed with worry. "What's happened?"

"Please," I implored. "Please. Let's walk. Don't—"

Then Jacques came up to us and he saw us and he stopped too, and said, "Why, Camilla!"

I didn't say anything; it was as though I had been struck mute, and I looked first at Jacques and then at Frank and my voice and my will were paralyzed.

"This must be Frank Rowan," Jacques said pleasantly. "I'm very glad to meet you. I'm Jacques Nissen."

"How do you do." Frank shook hands with Jacques, looking bewildered.

"How ravishing you look tonight, Camilla," Jacques said lightly. "I hope you've had a pleasant evening."

The gift of the tongue was returned to me. "Yes, thank you," I said.

"Well, good night, darling," Jacques said to me. "Good night, Frank."

"Good night," I said simultaneously with Frank, and then Jacques had moved on down the street.

"Camilla—" Frank said, and he looked suddenly helpless.

Then I said, because it was Frank I was with and I felt that I must tell him the truth now or he might misunderstand completely, "That was Jacques Nissen. He's—I saw him—" I started to tell Frank that I had seen Jacques kissing Mother, but I could not say that. "My mother's been seeing him," I said. "She's told him about you. She said she was never going to see him again. She lied."

"Maybe he went to see someone else."

"Maybe," I said, "but I don't think so. I think if he knew anybody else who lived here I'd know it. Anyhow, he knew who you were. He wouldn't have known who you were unless Mother'd told him. Frank, I don't want to go home."

"Listen," Frank said, "I'll walk all night with you if you want to, Camilla. But you go into the lobby first of all and telephone upstairs and tell your mother you're not coming home right now. I promised I'd bring you home and I don't want your parents forbidding you to see me. They might, you know."

"They can't keep me from seeing anybody I want to see."

"It'll be a lot easier if they don't think I'm leading you astray."

"What'll be easier?"

Frank grinned at me. "Leading you astray."

"Okay, I'll call Mother," I said.

I called on the house phone. Carter was evidently in early from her evening out and she answered it. I said, "I want to speak to Mother."

"Oh, it's you, Miss Camilla," Carter said. "What a shame you didn't get home a few minutes ago. Mr. Nissen has just left and he said he was so sorry to miss you."

How I hated Carter.

Mother came to the phone. "Camilla, darling, it's so late, I—where are you?"

"Downstairs."

"Well, darling, come up. It's past your bedtime."

"Where's Father?"

"He was detained. He won't be in till late."

"Oh," I said.

"Come up, darling. I want to hear all about your evening."

"Will you tell me all about yours?" I didn't know I could be so cold and horrible.

There was a sudden funny little silence. Then my mother's voice came breathless and somehow frightened. "Of course. Darling, why are you downstairs?"

"I just wanted to tell you I'm not coming up yet. I'm going for a walk."

"Alone? At this time of night? Camilla, please come upstairs right away, dear."

"I'm not alone," I said. "I'm with Frank. And I don't want to come up."

"But it's late. It's past your bedtime already. Your father will be terribly angry."

"I don't care," I said.

"He'll forbid you to see Frank, he'll—"

"I don't care what he does. I don't care."

Frank had been standing across the lobby so as not to eavesdrop on my conversation. Now he came over to me and said in a low voice, "Listen, Camilla, let's go upstairs. I'll go with you. It'll be better. Really."

On the other end of the phone my mother was saying, "Please, darling, please come upstairs. Please let me talk to you."

"All right!" I cried. "All right!" And I hung up.

Frank took my hand and held it tightly but he didn't say anything. We went up in the elevator and when I put my key to the lock my hand was trembling so that Frank took it from me and opened the door.

My mother was waiting for us and I think she was surprised to see Frank. She wore her rose velvet negligee and her hair was loose and she looked young and beautiful in spite of the anxiety on her face.

"Camilla, darling," she said, and then she smiled at Frank. "I'm so glad you came up, Frank. Now I'll really have a chance to see what you look like. There was such a mob this afternoon after the concert. . . ."

Frank held out his hand. "Good evening, Mrs. Dickinson. I'm very sorry I'm a little late in bringing Camilla home. She and David didn't get through their game as early as they'd expected."

"That's perfectly all right," my mother said. "Won't you come in, dear?"

"No, thank you. I have to get back downtown. Is it all right with you, Mrs. Dickinson, if I take Camilla out after school tomorrow afternoon and take her out to supper? I'll get her back early so she'll have plenty of time to do her homework."

"Well, yes," my mother said hesitantly. "I don't know—yes, I think it would be all right, Frank."

"Thanks a lot, Mrs. Dickinson. Good night. Good night, Cam."

Even in my blind rage at having seen Jacques coming out of the apartment something in me cried out in joy, I'm going to see Frank tomorrow!

Aloud I said, "Good night, Frank," and watched the door close behind him.

My mother put her arm on my shoulder and tried to draw me to her, but as she touched me I felt myself go rigid. It wasn't anything I wanted to do. It just happened.

"Darling," she said, "please come into my room and let's talk. Please."

I followed her into her room. She sat down on the chaise longue, tucking her feet up and hugging her knees. "Darling, sit down. Please."

I sat on her dressing table stool and waited. I didn't know what she was going to say and I knew that I couldn't say anything.

"You know that I was with Jacques tonight." She made it a statement, not a question.

"Yes."

"And you think it was a very terrible thing for me to do?"

"Yes," I said.

"Oh, darling, darling, don't condemn me for— I'm not wholly bad. I could be jealous of you because you're growing more beautiful every day, and you're young and I'm growing old and I can't expect my own beauty to last forever, and I've loved being beautiful, Camilla. I've loved it too much. If I didn't know I was beautiful I'd never have been able to believe your father loved me at all. If I weren't beautiful I'd be everything Rafferty despises. But I'm not jealous of you, darling, truly, truly I'm—a little sad, sometimes, maybe, because of myself, but never jealous."

"That doesn't have anything to do with Jacques," I said.

My mother seemed to wilt. "No," she said in a small voice. "No, I know." Then she said, "Darling, I—oh, darling, I know it looked awful but it wasn't as awful as it looked."

"Why not?" I asked.

"Because I'm going away, and after I go away I'm never going to see him again. I don't love Jacques, not the way I love Rafferty. And he knows that—I mean, Rafferty does."

"Then why do you see Jacques?"

"But I'm not. I mean—oh, darling, don't. You're so frightening sitting there and staring at me with those accusing green eyes. I thought—it seemed to me I ought to say good-bye to Jacques."

"Is this the first time you've seen him since—since the night you tried to kill yourself?"

"Oh, darling, don't say that—I don't think I ever really meant—I was half out of my mind that evening—"

"But is this the first time you've seen Jacques since then?" I asked.

"No," my mother said. "No—not quite—but almost —and after this—after next week I'll never see him again."

"Then why did you see him tonight?"

"I told you, darling—there are certain responsibilities —I thought I owed him at least a good-bye, after—"

"But, Mother," I asked, "if you knew you didn't love him, if you knew it was Father you loved, then why did you go on seeing him?"

All at once my mother looked exhausted. She leaned back against the chaise longue. "Oh, darling," she said, "you're too young to know anything about love. It isn't anything as—as simple as you think it is. It's the most horrible—the most complicated thing in the world."

"I don't think it's simple," I said.

"But you don't know," my mother said. "You have to be in love yourself before you could understand."

I am, I said to myself. I'm in love with Frank.

And suddenly I knew entirely and completely that this was true. David had seen it all along, but I only knew it now as I looked down at my mother's little puckered face, so small and childish, as she lay back against the chaise longue. Perhaps love in capital letters was complicated, but the fact that I was in love with Frank seemed suddenly the simplest and most inevitable thing in the world.

"Sometimes I think the world would run a lot better if it weren't for love," my mother went on, "but if it weren't for love I couldn't live. Your father could. That's where—that's where we're so different. He has his work, his buildings. Oh, Camilla darling, how jealous I've been of those buildings. I've been far more jealous of his buildings than I ever would have been of a woman. At least I could have understood the thing in a man that makes him love a woman."

"But Father loves you," I said flatly.

"Yes," my mother said. "I know he does. But I only know it once in a while, and then it's so wonderful I—I want—I need to know it all the time. And Jacques—"

"What about Jacques?" I asked in the same cold

voice with which I had been speaking to my mother and which I had never used to her before.

"Jacques—oh, darling, don't you see it isn't Jacques at all? It's just that Jacques gives me what I want from Rafferty. At first I thought it was Jacques—that I loved him—but now I know it was never Jacques. It was Rafferty all along."

"Mother," I said then, sharply, "you said you were going away. Where are you going?"

"Oh, darling, now Rafferty will be angry—but I suppose I must tell you, since I've gone this far. We're going to Italy."

"When?"

"Next week."

"But I don't want to go to Italy!" I cried. For the moment I forgot about Mother and Father and Jacques. All I could think of was that if I went to Italy I would not be able to see Frank.

My mother began pleating the rose-colored velvet of her negligee between her fingers. "That's just it, darling. Rafferty and I are going alone."

"Oh," I said, and I was immeasurably relieved.

"You see, darling," my mother went on, "we've been talking about you a great deal, Rafferty and I. We've both felt that you've changed this winter, that Luisa and Frank Rowan haven't been good for you—"

"It hasn't been Luisa and Frank," I said.

"But, darling, you *have* changed—and you've been just walking out of the house without telling us where

you were going and not coming home till all hours—
and you're not old enough yet—and you're always
with Luisa or now Frank—"

"It's not Luisa or Frank," I said again.

And my mother repeated, "But, darling, you *have*
changed."

And I thought angrily, Don't you know why? You,
of all people?

She knew, because she said then, "I know a lot of it
has been my fault. I don't think I ever should have had
children. I'm not—I couldn't ever be a really good
mother. I was—I was almost glad when I lost the baby
that came after you—it was only because I knew
Rafferty wanted another—"

"You didn't want me, did you?" I asked, still in that
strange cold voice that issued from my mouth but that
seemed to have nothing to do with me, to be no part
of Camilla Dickinson.

"Camilla!" my mother cried. "You mustn't say
things like that, ever! I love you—I love you more than
my life. How can you say I don't want you?"

"I don't mean you don't want me now," I said. "I
mean you didn't want me then."

My mother got up from the chaise longue and came
over to me and knelt down beside me. She put her
arms around me and began to kiss me with little
frantic kisses. "Darling," she said, "I couldn't ever
remember a time when I didn't want you, ever, ever,
ever." I let my head drop down onto her shoulder and
she said, "Camilla, do you mind too terribly about our

going to Italy, your father and I? It's—I think everything will be all right if we go away together—truly, truly, I think everything will be all right and I'll never make you suffer again the way I've made you suffer this winter. I do know that I've made you suffer, darling, that was one of the reasons I— Darling, I never *wanted* to make you suffer. You know that."

"I know," I said. "And it's all right about your going to Italy. I don't mind staying in New York."

"But, darling, you're not staying in New York."

"What do you mean?" I asked, jerking away.

"Well, darling, your father and I—I know it's partly my fault because I haven't been the kind of mother I should have been, but—you *have* been getting out of hand—and we thought it would be best if you went to a good boarding school for the rest of the year."

"No," I said, and stood up with such violence that my mother lost her balance and sat down on the carpet at my feet. She did not attempt to stand up, but sat there, reaching up to the hem of my skirt with her hand, like a little dressmaker.

"Darling, it's all decided. It's all settled," she said in a low voice.

"Couldn't you have consulted me?" I asked harshly.

My mother got up onto her knees again and it was almost as though she were praying to me as she said, "At first we talked about taking you with—and then I thought it would be better if we went alone—and better for you, too, in the end, darling. And Rafferty thought so too. He thought you weren't quite ready

241

to come with us. And we thought you'd enjoy boarding school."

"I don't want to leave New York," I said. "I like the school I'm at now. Please get a governess or a companion or something for me and let me stay here. Please, Mother!" My voice rose in urgency and now I was praying down at her as she knelt there on the carpet.

But she said, "Camilla, oh, my darling baby, there's nothing in the world I can do about it. I'd like to give you anything in the world you want, you know that. But Rafferty and—it's just that it's all settled."

"You mean you're sending me away just because of Frank and Luisa?"

"That's part of it—but just in general—your father and I thought it would be what you needed. We thought you'd like it. Most girls are terribly excited about going to boarding school."

Perhaps I might have been a year ago, or six months ago. But I hadn't met Frank then. I hadn't learned then what it was like to be in love. I didn't know much about boarding schools but I didn't think there was much place for love in them. And no place for Frank.

My mother stood up and said, "Darling, it's terribly late. You should have been in bed long ago, and there's school tomorrow. You can try to talk to your father if you want to tomorrow—but it won't do any good."

She was right. It would do no good. It was all settled. I would have to go. I said, "Good night," and went back to my room.

I undressed and got into bed and I couldn't sleep. I lay there and there was nothing but a great ache over all of me because now I would have to leave New York and perhaps Frank would never kiss me. I got out of bed and went over to the window and the black shocking night air rushed at me and I wanted to burst into tears, to cry loudly, loudly, as I might have not so many years ago when I was still a child. But I just stood still, by the window, and then I slammed the window down and leaned my forehead against the cold glass and looked out into the courtyard. On the roof of the apartment house across the way I saw a shadow moving and then I realized that there was someone leaning against the parapet. As I became more accustomed to the dark I saw that it was a woman and she was just leaning there, quite quietly; and suddenly she flung her arms out in a gesture of despair or anger and turned around and went back in. There was an oblong of yellow light as she opened the door that led back into the house, and then darkness again as it closed behind her. I stood there a moment longer and then went back to bed. I thought, I will see Frank tomorrow.

I lay there and I held on to the thought of Frank like someone in a boundless ocean holding on to a spar of wood. It was the only thing that kept me from going under the cold dark waters. The land behind me was gone, and I could not see the land ahead, but the knowledge that I would see Frank the next day kept me afloat.

10

The next morning Luisa was not at school. Luisa is never ill and I worried about her off and on when I wasn't worrying about myself and my own problems. As soon as school was over I hurried down to the coatroom. Frank was waiting just outside the door for me. I jumped when I saw him though I had been hoping that possibly, possibly he might be there —even though I knew his school let out later than ours.

"Hi," he said.

"Hi. What's wrong with Luisa?" Then I saw that Frank looked unusually solemn and my heart jumped within me in fear like a fish leaping out of water.

Frank took my hand and we started walking down the street. "Mona kept Luisa at home today to talk to her. I don't know just what about. But there was certainly a mess at our apartment last night, Camilla.

I hope you never have to go through a mess like it. Not that Luisa and I were supposed to go through it, but when Mona and Bill have a little discussion, nobody in the neighborhood's likely to get much sleep. Anyhow, I cut trigonometry this afternoon because I wanted to talk to you. Bill's firm wants to send him to Cincinnati."

"Oh," I said, and the fear stayed in my heart as I waited for Frank to continue.

"I don't know whether he's going or not. I think it means a good raise in salary and we could certainly use it, except that it would mean Mona would have to give up her job on the magazine and she doesn't want to do that."

I nodded. I knew that the magazine was more than a job to Mona; it was some kind of symbol.

"I think Bill should go to Cincinnati," Frank continued. "His job—well, it hasn't been much of anything, up to now. Maybe it's paid for food and rent but it certainly hasn't paid for anything else. Mona's sent Luisa and me to school; sometimes I think she's done it just to spite Bill, so he'd feel he couldn't take care of his own kids. Luisa and I could have gone to public school perfectly well. And Mona pays for our clothes and of course her own, and every time she buys a shirt or a tie or a pair of pajamas for Bill she lets him know he wouldn't have a stitch of clothes on his back if it weren't for her. That's a lousy position to put a man in and Mona's a fool to do it."

Frank spoke in a quiet, dispassionate voice, and I felt

that again I was learning, that I would have to try to think about my parents with the same loving objectivity. Because there was no question about it: Frank loved Mona and Bill.

He said, "Sometimes I think some devil in Mona just deliberately makes her do the things that will make Bill resent her most. Anyhow, I think he should go to Cincinnati and take Mona with him."

"What about you and Luisa?" I asked.

"Well, I suppose we'd have to go too. I don't want to, but I think we owe it to Bill."

"I'm going away too," I said in a low voice, looking down at the sidewalk, and it seemed to me that now everything was over, over, that just as my life was beginning, everything in it that I cared about was coming to an end.

"You? Where?" Frank asked in a startled way.

I continued to look down at the sidewalk. "Mother and Father are going to Italy for the rest of the winter. So I'm going to some boarding school."

"When?" Frank asked.

"Soon. Next week, I think."

Frank said what I had been thinking. "Winter's just started and now all of a sudden it's almost over. Or it's been stopped and we have to start it all over again somewhere else. And I liked the way it was starting right here. I wish it didn't have to change."

"So do I," I whispered, because I was very near to crying.

Then Frank seemed to throw his shoulders back and

246

stand up taller. "Well, if you're going off next week, we have this week. Let's make it a wonderful week, Cam. Let's see each other every day. Okay? Shall we make it the week of Camilla and Frank?"

"Yes," I said, feeling suddenly happy again. Even if Bill and Mona were taking Frank and Luisa to Cincinnati, even if Mother and Father were going to Italy and sending me to boarding school, Frank and I would have a week together. And it was not only that we would have the week, but that it had been Frank's idea. He might be leaving New York forever but I was the one he wanted to spend his last week with. I was so happy I wanted to throw my head back and sing loudly with the joy of a rooster greeting the morning.

"What shall we do, Cam?" Frank asked me. "I haven't got much money so it can't be anything too terrific, but shall we ride on the Staten Island Ferry? That's one of the classic things."

"Yes, let's," I said.

"Do you know Edna Saint Vincent Millay?" he asked me. "I should think you might like her. I feel I've outgrown her but there's one thing kind of apropos right now. *We were very young, we were very merry, we rode back and forth all night on the ferry*. I like that. So we'll just ride over and back and then think of something else to do. I wish I could take you for a ride in one of the hansom cabs in Central Park but I'm afraid I couldn't quite swing that."

"I'd rather ride on the ferry, anyhow," I said, though

I would have adored to ride in a hansom cab with Frank.

It was a gray day with misty clouds hanging low over the city and it was already beginning to get dark when we got on the ferry. One or two soft feathers of snow came dropping slowly out of the sky but it wasn't really snowing. Frank and I went directly to the bow of the boat and stood there looking out over the water. You could somehow tell just by the look of the water that it was terribly deep, that it was so deep that great steamships could navigate in it. It was an iron-gray color and the little waves had somehow the quality of metal. A raw wind was blowing and I put the collar of my coat up.

"Are you cold?" Frank asked me. "Want to go inside?"

"No. No, I like it out here."

The ferry started moving with a jerk that threw me against Frank. He put his arm around me and we stood there that way, as the ferry pushed out into the dark gray water. As we moved, the mist thickened and we could see nothing but water and then a thick soft blanket of fog and we might have been going out into the open sea; we could see nothing ahead of us. We looked back and behind us the skyline of New York was disappearing into the fog. It was like a mirage or a city in a fairy tale put under a spell and disappearing forever into the mist.

Frank dropped his arm from my waist and said abruptly, "You know, Cam, about God."

"What?" I asked, startled.

"You know what we need is a new God." I didn't say anything, so after a moment he went on. "I mean, what we need is a God people like me, or David, or you, or our parents, could really believe in. I mean, look at all the advances we've made scientifically since —oh, well, since Christ was born if you want to put a date on it. Transportation—look how that's changed. And communication. Telegraph and telephones and television. They're all new and a few thousand years ago we couldn't even have conceived of them but now we can't conceive of doing without them. But you take God. God hasn't changed any since Jesus took him out of a white nightgown and long whiskers. You know what I mean. Along about when Christ was born, just a few years A.D., it was time someone should conceive a new God and then have the power to give his new understanding to the world. So what we need again now is a new God. The God most people are worshiping in churches and temples hasn't grown since Christ's time. He's deteriorated. Look what the Middle Ages did to the Church. All this arguing about how many angels could stand on the point of a needle. All the velvet and gold on the outside and decadence on the inside. And then the Victorians. They tried to put God back in a long white nightgown and whiskers again. That kind of a God isn't any good for today.

You can't blame Mona for not believing in that kind of God. We need a God who's big enough for the atomic age."

He stopped for a moment, staring out over the water into the fog, and then he said, "Listen, maybe all that sounds awfully arrogant. But it isn't all mine. I mean, an awful lot of it I got from David. But I thought out something myself that I think's kind of good, only I don't really believe in it. If I *did* believe in it I think it would be the most logical kind of explanation for things. I mean, I think it would satisfy me. But just because I thought of it myself I can't have faith in it. You know, Cam, we live on a pretty stinking little planet in a second-rate little constellation in a backwash of the universe."

"Yes, I know," I said.

"And when you think of all the millions of stars your astronomers see and then all the millions of stars that must be out there somewhere beyond the reach of even the most gigantic telescope that could ever be invented, who are we to say that there aren't stars or planets somewhere else with life on them, and life much better than ours? Why should the Earth, which is, as I said—well, it isn't even second-rate, it's lower than that—why should the Earth be the only planet with life on it when you think of stars and constellations and everything going on forever and ever and ever? I mean, you take space, and space goes on and on and on. And does it end the way Einstein says it does? And if it does, what's beyond that? So what I figured out was this: nobody ever gets a chance to finish on this Earth. And even if there's a heaven nobody's good enough at the end of life on this Earth to be ready to go to heaven. In the first place, we haven't got the equipment. And I don't think it's fair of God to give us brains to ask questions if He isn't going to let us answer them sometimes. So I figured that when we die, maybe we go to another planet, the next planet in the scale. Maybe we get better brains there that will make us able to learn and understand just a little more than anyone—even someone like Einstein—is able to understand on this Earth. And maybe we might get another sense. I mean, maybe before we got born on the Earth we were on another planet where no one could see. If everybody in the world was born blind, if there wasn't any such thing as sight, we wouldn't have the slightest idea what it was. We couldn't conceive of it even in our wildest dreams. So maybe on the next planet there's a new sense, just as important as sight, or even more important, but which we can't conceive of now any more than we could conceive of sight if we didn't know about it. And then when we'd finished on that planet we'd go on to another planet and develop even more, and so on and on and on, for hundreds and thousands or maybe even millions of planets, learning and growing all the time, until at last we'd finally know and understand everything—absolutely everything—and then maybe we'd be ready for heaven.

"I guess when you're ready for heaven you're able to

stop caring about being an individual. And I don't think I could ever stop caring about being an individual unless I'd lived billions and billions of years and really *did* know and understand everything. I mean, then maybe I'd be ready for God."

"I think that's wonderful!" I cried. "Oh, Frank, I think it's wonderful. I could believe in something like that. I should think anyone could. Did you tell Luisa?"

"Her?" Frank asked scornfully. "She just said she was fed up hearing me talk about the importance of Frank Rowan and thinking of a system where Frank Rowan could go on being important. I didn't mean it that way."

"Oh, Frank," I said. Then I asked, "Did you—did you talk to David about it?"

"Yes," Frank said. "Yes. David was very nice. He liked the idea. But I could tell that he didn't believe in it. Maybe even he thought I was caring too much about being Frank Rowan at all costs again. I don't know. He was just very nice and—and sort of sad."

We were beginning to see Staten Island now, looming up out of the fog. Frank said, "I told Pompilia Riccioli and she laughed. She just sat down and laughed till the tears rolled down her cheeks. You're the only person who seems to have cared in the right way, Camilla."

"I do care," I told him. "I care awfully."

Now we drew into the Staten Island slip and Frank took my arm and held it very tight and we walked off the ferry into the cold damp air of Staten Island.

"Want to go somewhere and have a frankfurter or something?" Frank asked.

But I wasn't hungry. I shook my head. "No. But you go on and have something if you want to."

"Me, you think I could eat?" Frank turned on me and his voice was suddenly savage. "You think I could eat when the minute you're born you're condemned to die? When thousands of people are dying every minute before they've even had a chance to begin? Death isn't fair. It's—it's a denial of life! How can we be given life when we're given death at the same time? Death isn't fair," Frank cried again, his voice soaring and cracking with rage. "I resent death! I resent it with every bone in my body! And you think—you think I could eat!"

He looked at me as though he hated me. He jammed a coin into the slot and pushed me ahead of him onto the New York–bound ferry and stood with his arms crossed in bitter and passionate anger. He did not look at me; he did not talk. Once when the ferry slapped into a wave and I was thrown against him he pulled away from me as though I repelled him. I had heard Luisa talk about Frank's moods and I supposed that this was one of them, but it frightened me. I stood there beside him and as many millions of miles away from him as one of the planets he had been talking about and tried not to shiver. It was not because I was cold that I was shivering, but because of Frank.

There wasn't any choice anymore. I couldn't say any longer, even to myself, I don't think I'll grow up for a while yet; I think I'll be a child just a little longer. Being a child was something that I was afraid to let go of but that now I had to let go of, because I knew that if I loved Frank I could no longer be a child.

A sudden gust of wind lifted my beret from my head and flung it into the water. Frank did not appear to notice and I knew that if I should cry out "Oh, my hat" or anything, it would anger him even more. So I just stood there beside him and let the wind push my hair back from my forehead and drive my breath back down into my throat, almost choking me. And there was Frank standing beside me consumed with rage and I was afraid.

Then as the towers of New York began to be visible through the fog I could feel Frank slowly beginning to relax. The terrible tenseness left his body and all of a sudden he said in quite a happy voice, "You know what, Cam, there's something awfully exciting about New York even if you've been born and brought up in it."

"I think it's even more exciting if you've been born and brought up in it. I think it's the most exciting place in the world to call home," I said, but even though Frank had relaxed I was still caught up in the tenseness of his rage.

We left the ferry and started to walk through the downtown streets. They were filling up now with people leaving the business district and getting ready to go home, and the next ferry would be a great deal more crowded than the one we had ridden on. A sharp wind was blowing and I wished my beret were not somewhere in the cold waters but on my cold head instead. Frank took my arm and we pushed through the streets until the crowds began to diminish and we were on a quiet street with only one or two other people walking quickly, heads bowed to the wind.

I walked along beside Frank and my own happy mood had gone and I wanted to cry out to him, "Say something comforting!" though I did not know what there was that he could say. Frank and Luisa would be going to Cincinnati and I would be going to boarding school and everything would be over, over. And all because of Jacques, I thought, forgetting in my misery that Jacques had nothing to do with Cincinnati; all because of my father's not—I did not know exactly what it was that my father had not done that he ought to have done, but I knew it was something; all because of my mother's weeping and sobbing one afternoon and then trying so foolishly to cut her wrists, and why? I knew my mother did not want to die.

"Frank," I asked, "what would you think of someone who tried to commit suicide?" The wind blew a bitter gust and my words seemed forced back into my throat, as though they would have been better unsaid.

Frank grabbed me by both arms. "Camilla, you're not—"

"No, it isn't me," I said. "I'm not talking about myself."

"But you're talking about someone," Frank stated flatly.

"Well—you can't talk about no one, can you?"

Frank continued to hold my arms. He looked sternly down into my eyes. "I think it's the unforgivable sin, Camilla. If God gave us life He didn't mean us to try to fling His gift back in His teeth. Suicide is murder."

"You don't think it could ever be right, ever?"

"No," Frank said. And then he said. "Oh, Cam, I don't know. You aren't talking about David, are you?"

"No."

"Because I don't think it would be all right for him, and I don't think he does, either."

"I wasn't talking about David," I said. The wind penetrated my clothes, through my skin and into my bones. My veins seemed to be running with wind rather than blood.

"The way Johnny's older brother died—it was suicide in a way, I suppose. He died in order to save the rest of his crew. Oh, Cam, all I know is, there isn't any one answer to any question. Cam, why did you ask me about suicide?"

"I—I don't know," I said.

"Cam, I don't want ever to pry, but—but you worry me when you talk about things like that."

"It was my mother," I said then, and the wind sent a shiver through me. "My mother tried to—a couple of weeks ago."

"Cam," Frank said, and his fingers tightened about my arms so that they dug through my coat into my skin.

"Frank," I said, "I don't understand about people when they're really grown-up. I don't understand my mother or my father. I see certain things—and I remember other things—and all of it's just enough to confuse me."

"I know," Frank said, "I know, Cam darling." It was the first time he had ever called me anything except Camilla or Cam, and there was that word "darling" again, such a common, overused word, and now all of a sudden it was as though it had never been used before, as though David had never said it, or my mother, or Luisa in her sarcastic way. Now it was a completely new word, born for the first time as Frank said it out on the windy street; and it was like a caress; in spite of the cold I felt the same warm glow all through me that I had felt when David passed his hand over my hair, and I wanted to fling my arms about Frank and cry, "Oh, Frank, kiss me, kiss me."

But Frank took his hands away from my elbows and dug them down into the pockets of his coat and said, "Sometimes I've worried horribly that Mona might try to kill herself. Some nights when Luisa and I've heard her crying all night long I've thought she might just go out of her mind and do something desperate, but she never did."

We started to walk again and the warm glow left me, and my feet and fingers and my ears ached with cold.

We passed a church and Frank said, "Camilla, you're frozen, aren't you? Let's go in for a minute and get warm."

It was a small church, and inside the air smelled

heavy and dusty and the light was dim, and dusty too. We walked in together, quietly, and went in to one of the pews and sat down. Being in a church with Frank was very different from being in one with Mother and Father, or Binny or the governess who had taken me when I was younger. Being in church with Frank was being much closer to God in the house of God than I had ever been before. We sat there for quite a while and I began to unfreeze and to be happy again. I don't know what Frank was thinking, but I was thinking about what he had said about going on to different planets and learning and growing and improving, and it seemed terribly right to me, and I felt, too, oh, yes, God is here, this is God's house.

I looked around. Although there was no service going on, there was somehow a lingering smell of incense in the musty air, and the light came through the stained-glass windows warm and beautiful and unlike the gray air outside.

Frank leaned toward me once and whispered, "Camilla, if people can make things as beautiful as churches why can't they make a God worthy of a church?"

"I don't know," I whispered back.

"Maybe David has the right answer," Frank said. "He told me once something of Montaigne's that I've never been able to forget. 'Oh, senseless man, who cannot possibly make a worm, and yet will make Gods by dozens.' But look at Jesus. I don't think Montaigne was talking about Jesus."

"No," I said. We were silent again then. Once I looked at Frank, and his face was very stern and I wondered whether or not he was praying. I didn't really pray myself. I just kept saying over and over to God, Make it always be like this with Frank and me. Make us know each other always.

We got up to leave and just as we got to the outside doors a gray-haired lady in expensive furs came in and she looked at me and said, "Oh, dear, you didn't go into the church without a hat, did you?"

"Yes," I said, remembering my red beret drowning in New York Harbor.

"But you know you mustn't ever go into a church without covering your head, dear," the lady said. "Didn't your mother teach you that?"

"Yes," I said. I felt Frank stiffen with rage beside me.

"I am so sorry," Frank said, his voice soaring and then cracking down onto a deep note, "that you object to Miss Dickinson's going into a church without her hat. However, I'm sure that God doesn't object, and after all, that's all that matters." And he swept me out.

Something about Frank's wrath, so ridiculous, so rude, and so right, struck me as funny, and I began to giggle. I was afraid to look at him for fear I'd make him even angrier; and then my giggles turned into laughter and then beside me I heard Frank laughing, too, and the two of us walked down the street roaring with laughter. We laughed and laughed until the tears were rolling down our cheeks and we were staggering like drunks. And then there on the empty street Frank had his arms around me again and our cheeks were pressed together and our laughter vanished, and we stood there holding each other terribly tightly, as though we were afraid somebody would come walking down the street to wrench us apart. We stood there clutching each other and I could feel Frank's cheek against mine, cold and just faintly rough; and it seemed to me that if he let go of me I would fall down to the pavement and not be able to rise until he lifted me up.

Then he said, "Oh, Cam," and again, "Oh, Cam," and we moved apart, very slowly, and started walking again. We didn't talk for several blocks and then Frank said, in a numbed kind of voice, "We'll have to eat now, and then I'll have to take you back home or they won't let us spend the rest of the week together. I'll come for you tomorrow after school. If we're going to Cincinnati it doesn't matter if I miss a few classes now. I don't care, anyhow. And I'm going to ask Bill for five bucks. I've never asked him for anything before, but I'm going to now."

"Frank," I said, "I never have anything to spend my allowance on. I've got quite a lot saved. Please let me lend you the five dollars. I'd much rather have you borrow it from me than from Bill."

Frank didn't say anything and I was afraid I'd made him angry again, but at last he took my hand in his. "Okay, Cam. Thanks. I think I'd rather borrow from you than from Bill too. But it's just a loan. Understand that."

"I do," I said. "I do understand, Frank."

"Tomorrow we'll go to the Planetarium, maybe. Would you like that?"

"Yes," I said. "I want to go to the Planetarium with you."

"I want to do everything in the world with you," Frank said. "You're the only person in the world I've ever felt that way about. Cam, I've never talked to anybody the way I've talked to you. I've never wanted to. What a lot of time we've wasted. We haven't even known each other two weeks. Why didn't we know each other before?"

"I don't know."

"It's Luisa," Frank said. "Of course it's Luisa. Luisa's the most possessive person I've ever known. She's even more possessive than Mona. Take those dolls of hers. The only reason she's hung on to them as long as she has is that they're her possessions and she can't bear to part with anything that belongs to her. The way she's always talked about you, you'd have thought she made you up. And I must say she made you sound sort of a dope. I should have known I'd have to talk to you for myself to see what you were like. Oh, Camilla. I'll be glad when I'm twenty-one. Parents can certainly mess up our lives, can't they? If it weren't for parents I wouldn't be going to Cincinnati and you wouldn't be going to boarding school. And I don't believe they think about us at all when they get involved in all these messes. We're just something that has to be disposed of like their furniture or clothing. I suppose Mona'll load all the furniture into a van and the clothes into trunks, and Luisa and I'll be loaded into a train and that will be that. Nobody's worrying about whether Luisa and I are having fits about leaving New York and having our whole lives disrupted. If we were just a few years older I'd say to heck with them, let's get married; but we're not. Here, we'll go in here and eat and then I'll take you home."

Somehow neither of us had anything to say while we ate or on the way back to the apartment. At the door Frank took both my hands and held them tight and said, "Until tomorrow, Cam," and he left me.

I went upstairs and I thought that it was the most wonderful day I had ever had, and when I thought of the way Frank and I had held each other there on the deserted street my legs felt all weak beneath me. It wasn't until I was in bed that night that I remembered that he hadn't kissed me.

II

The next day I got to school almost an hour early because somehow that seemed to bring me closer to the time when I would see Frank, and it seemed as though I could not exist until school was out. I didn't know that a day could go so slowly. I'd read of minutes seeming like hours but until that day I'd thought it was an exaggeration; a minute was a minute even in the waiting room of a dentist's office, and that was that. Now I realized that time has very little to do with the clock; it's all inside you. Each minute that morning stretched out interminably; it was like walking down a long dark corridor with only a dim light in the distance to tell you it would ever end. But the times when I was with Frank an hour would slip by like a leaf dropping from a tree.

I was stupid that morning too. I looked at Luisa's

empty desk and wondered how soon they would be leaving for Cincinnati and whether or not she was helping Mona pack, and I answered idiotically when it was my turn to recite until finally Miss Sargent asked if I was feeling well.

The instant the last bell rang I fled to the coatroom and grabbed my coat and an old red velvet beret of Mother's she had loaned me until she had time to get me a new one. I was out of breath when I reached the door, partly from hurrying, and partly from excitement.

Frank was not there.

For a moment my heart seemed to stop beating. Then I tried to control my fear, to tell myself that I was being stupid, that the day before I hadn't hurried as much, I'd taken longer in the coatroom; Frank would be there in a moment. I looked up and down the street—I didn't know from which direction he would approach—and I kept thinking that I saw him, but it was always someone older or younger or shorter or fatter or dark-haired or blond; it was never Frank.

Then I told myself that perhaps he had not been able to cut his last class as he had the day before. After all, cutting classes is not an easy thing to do. Perhaps his absence the day before had been noticed and they were making sure that he didn't get off early again. That seemed to me to be a very logical explanation of why he was not there waiting for me, and I leaned back against the side of the building to wait for him. One by one the other girls came out and started down the street, calling, "Good-bye." "Who're you waiting for, Camilla?" "See you tomorrow." I called good-bye to them all, though I was scarcely conscious of my voice coming from my throat.

"Good-bye, good-bye," I called, and looked anxiously down the street.

Last of all Miss Sargent came out and paused as she saw me standing there. "Waiting for someone, Camilla?"

"Yes, Miss Sargent."

"Sure you feel all right today? You seemed very restless."

"Oh, I'm fine, thank you, Miss Sargent."

"What's the matter with Luisa? A cold?"

"No. I think her family's going to move to Cincinnati and she's helping her mother pack."

"Oh?" Miss Sargent asked. "It's odd that Mrs. Rowan hasn't communicated with us here at the school. She sent a note saying that Luisa wouldn't be in for a couple of days, but that was all. Well, don't stay out in the cold too long. We don't want you coming down with one of those grippy colds everybody seems to be having."

I sighed with relief as she left me.

I waited out on the street until my teeth were chattering. Then I went back into the coatroom and waited there by the window where I could see anybody coming up or down the street, until the janitor stuck his head in the door and said, "I'm sorry, miss, but all you young ladies are supposed to be out of the building this time of day. I'm afraid I'll have to ask you to leave."

I stood out on the street again, and at last I realized all through me that Frank was not going to come. I walked until I reached a drugstore and went into a phone booth.

"Carter," I cried, "has anyone telephoned me? Has there been a message?"

"No, miss," Carter said. "Nobody's called at all except Mr. Nissen for your mother."

I hardly noticed her maliciousness. "Thank you," I said, and hung up.

Then I went down to Ninth Street. I did not want to go down to Ninth Street, looking for Frank, after he had left me waiting without a word, after he had not come as he had promised, but I could not help myself.

I pushed the buzzer to the Rowan apartment and when the door clicked open I started walking up the stairs. Oscar barked and barked and no one screamed at him to shut up and no one leaned over the banisters to ask who it was. The door to the apartment was open and Luisa and Mona both stood in the center of the room looking somehow lost and as though they were strangers in an alien place.

I stood in the doorway looking at them, and they looked at me, and no one said anything until I asked, "Where's Frank?"

A gleam came into Luisa's eye and when she spoke her voice sounded almost like Carter's telling me that no one had phoned except Jacques for mother. "He's gone," Luisa said.

I could only echo "Gone?" in a stupid sort of way.

"With Bill," Luisa said. "To Cincinnati. They left this morning."

"Oh," I said. My eyes searched the room as though, if I looked hard enough, I would surely see Frank somewhere.

I stood there, unable to move, until Luisa said, "Well, see you at school tomorrow." And then, as though in answer to a question, "Mona and I aren't going to Cincinnati. We're staying here."

"Oh," I said again.

Mona turned away then, with an impatient, angry gesture, but Luisa kept on looking at me with a horrible grimacing smile until I turned and left the room and started down the stairs. I was all the way downstairs and almost at the door when I heard Luisa's feet stampeding in a wild rush down the stairs and she flung herself at me, nearly knocking me over, and burst into tears. We stood there clutching each other and Luisa cried loudly with huge tearing sobs as though she hoped that the weeping would break her body into a thousand pieces. I stood with my arms around her while she almost screamed with sobs.

Then the door opened and two women came in and stared at us curiously before they started up the stairs. Luisa broke from me, her sobs slapped away by the presence of the women, and ran up the stairs, pushing ahead of them. I stood there in the hall until I heard

267

Oscar bark as Luisa banged on the door; and then the bark was silenced as the door slammed behind her.

I turned and left the apartment and started walking toward Sixth Avenue. I would have liked to cry as Luisa had cried, but whatever it is that governs one's control would not release its hold. My eyes stung, they were so dry, and the sharp December wind blowing in from the Hudson burned my face.

I didn't know what to do or where to go. I could not go home. Mother thought that I was out with Frank and I knew that I could not bear her questions or, what would be infinitely worse, her pity. Finally I went uptown, to Central Park, to the obelisk where I had met Frank. It was almost dark. A few mothers and nursemaids were taking children home to dinner; a few kids were still playing around. The sky was that color that is partly blue and partly green and that seems lit from inside by a special radiance; and the bare branches of the trees were delicate and lacy against it. In the few puddles at the sides of the walks a thin black lace of ice was forming.

Then I thought of David. Perhaps David would help me.

But when I got to Perry Street I almost didn't ring David's bell. I felt now that I couldn't talk to anybody in the world. And then, just as I had decided that I would go away, that I would just walk and walk until my mind cleared, I raised my hand and pushed the bell.

After a moment Mrs. Gauss opened the door and she

did not seem pleased to see me. She stood in the doorway, saying nothing, staring at me with unfriendly eyes, until I asked, "May I see David, please?"

"I think you'd better not," she said. "He isn't expecting you, is he? He didn't say anything to me about it."

"No," I said, "but—"

"It's very hard on him when people come unexpectedly," she said. "He likes to know beforehand."

"I'm sorry," I said, and turned to go.

But David's voice called, "Ma, who are you talking to?"

"It's just the superintendent," she said. "Now, don't you worry, Davy boy."

I looked at Mrs. Gauss, my mouth open with indignation. "But—" I started.

David called. "If it's Mrs. Tortaglia I want to see her."

"She can't come now. She's very busy," Mrs. Gauss called back.

"Send her in!" David called, his voice full of angry command.

Mrs. Gauss started to push me toward the door, but I was filled with sudden anger, and I broke away from her and ran past her into David's room.

David was in his chair and when he saw me he said, "Mrs. Tortaglia, eh? I thought so."

Mrs. Gauss had followed me to the doorway and stood there behind me, glaring. I was frightened, but my anger and my need to talk to David were still greater than my fear.

"Okay, Ma," David said. "Never were any good as a liar. Camilla isn't going to tire me. Go in the kitchen and have a glass of wine and cheer up."

She shot me another angry look and left us.

"Sorry, honey," David said. "Don't let her upset you. Thought she was keeping you away for my good. After you left on Sunday, had what I suppose you'd call a relapse. Got into a depression she thought would drive me out of my mind or kill me outright. Just crawling out of it, and since it happened after you were here, she blames it on you. Sorry she was rude to you. But don't judge her too harshly."

"I shouldn't have come," I said. "I just—"

David shut the book he had been reading and put it down on the table by him. "Loves me too much, that's all," he said. "Wants to protect me. Can't get it through her head the last thing I want is protection. Glad you came tonight, Camilla. Won't be bad for me. Won't get into one of my gruesome glooms. Wasn't really you, anyhow. Just me, myself, and I, one of the lousiest trios I know anything about." Then he looked at me sharply. "What's the matter? She frighten you?"

"No," I said. "It's not that."

"Something's happened to upset you. What is it?"

"It's just—" I started, but I couldn't tell him. I couldn't tell him that Frank had gone, and without a word, without a word.

And then David said, "Upset about Frank's leaving? It's too bad, but it was inevitable. Not so much the Cincinnati deal, but that Mona and Bill should break

270

up. Frank got over for a few minutes this morning to say good-bye. All pretty sudden, wasn't it?"

"Yes," I said, and I must have looked as though David had slapped me, because he asked, very gently, "Camilla, didn't Frank say good-bye to you?"

"No."

David reached out and took my hand and pulled me toward him and I dropped to my knees by his chair because my legs would not hold me up. He pulled me even closer to him so that my head rested against the hardness of his chest, and he said softly, "Camilla, don't judge Frank harshly. Everybody sometimes behaves in ways that are completely unexplainable, even to himself. Frank would never have hurt you deliberately."

But I knew now that nothing David could say would comfort me. Now I remembered Pompilia Riccioli and the little Italian girls, and that Frank had found time to say good-bye to David, but he had not cared enough about me to say good-bye to me.

Then David pressed his lips against my hair and then he raised my face and kissed my mouth, but this time I felt no lovely warmth flowing through me, only a deep numbing ache that seemed to paralyze my whole body.

David sighed. "Can't help you, can I, Camilla? Can't help you at all."

I shook my head and struggled to my feet.

David said, "You'll get over it. Know that, don't you, Camilla?"

"No," I said.

David said, "Right now you don't want to get over it, do you? But whether you want to or not, you will. That's the hell of it."

"I have to go now," I said.

"Where are you going?"

"I don't know. Just somewhere. To walk."

"Camilla," David said, catching me by the hand and pulling me toward him again, "you know Frank was just the first one for you, don't you? Believe me, believe me, it's best this way, without bitterness. Had a beautiful thing together, you and Frank; now it's ended, through neither of your faults, so you'll always have it. No one can take it away from you."

But there is bitterness, I thought. There is bitterness. Frank left and he didn't say good-bye to me. He didn't care enough to say good-bye.

"It's when someone you've loved tries to make the beautiful thing there's been between you into nothing, tries to deny it, that you lose it. You and Frank will always possess what you've had together even if you never meet again. Probably more if you never meet again."

"Good-bye," I said.

David sighed again. "Okay, honey. Know you can't listen to me. Come and see your old Uncle David soon, will you?"

"Yes," I said, though I knew that seeing David would always hurt because he was somehow part of Frank, and also because it was with Frank and me the way David had said it wasn't. By not caring enough even to say good-bye to me Frank had destroyed everything. All I wanted now was to forget him, though I knew that wasn't possible. And now I was glad I was going to boarding school.

I left David and walked over to the Stephanowskis' music shop, but there were several people standing around waiting to be helped. Mrs. Stephanowski excused herself from a man in a derby hat and hurried over to me, taking both my hands in hers.

"So Franky's left," she exclaimed, "and your little heart is sore. I know, darling, I know."

"Do you?" I asked. "David thinks I'm too young to have it really matter."

"Of course you're not too young," she said. "Of course it really matters. I wish I could talk to you now, but look at all these people. . . ." Mrs. Stephanowski looked at me with a worried expression. "Will you come to dinner tomorrow?"

"Yes," I said. "Thank you."

"Franky came by this morning to say good-bye to us. It's a bad thing he's going through."

"Yes," I said, but I had no room in me for pity for Frank. Had he said good-bye to Pompilia Riccioli, too, and all the others Mona preferred to Camilla Dickinson because they were at least human?

Mrs. Stephanowski had to go back to her customers. I stood there for a moment listening to music pouring in a confused blur of sound from the listening booths; then I turned and left the shop.

I stood there for a moment on the street, and finally

I started to walk uptown. Night was all about me and the city was ugly to me and dirty and I felt as though my heart inside me were bleeding and if it would only bleed enough I would die and I could think of nothing more beautiful than to die. And I thought of how angry Frank would be, of how he had shaken me when I said in the top balcony at the movies that I wanted to die, and then I walked several blocks doing nothing but keeping myself from crying openly on the street.

I wanted to walk all the way home. I thought that if I could walk all the way home there would be nothing left in me but tiredness, and I would be able to get into bed and sleep. But it was too far. My legs began to buckle under me, so I took a subway.

I knew when I got home that Jacques was there with my mother. I knew and I didn't care. The doorman said, "Good evening, Miss Camilla," and smiled at me with the eager and curious smile that no longer had the power to make me writhe inside.

I stepped into the elevator and the elevator boy said, as though he had something exotic-tasting in his mouth, "Good afternoon, Miss Camilla. You have company upstairs."

"Oh," I said.

"That Mr. Nissen is upstairs. He asked especially if you was in and then he said he'd go upstairs and wait for you."

So the elevator boy looked at me with that giggly look and let me out on the fourteenth floor, which is really the thirteenth floor. I pulled my key out of the pocket of my navy blue coat and let myself into the apartment. I could hear their voices in the living room. My mother came out to meet me.

"Camilla," she said, "we've been worried."

"Why?"

"Luisa's waiting in your room for you."

"I don't want to see Luisa," I said. "I don't want to see anybody."

"Oh, my darling," my mother said, "I know how unhappy you are about Frank's going to Cincinnati, but think how much worse it is for Luisa and Mrs. Rowan. After all, to lose a son or a brother is—and you're so young, darling. Just wait till you get away to boarding school and start having fun with the other girls. Darling, you'll get over it. I promise you. You always believe Mother when she makes a promise, don't you?"

"No," I said.

A sudden darkness flickered over my mother's face. Then she drew herself up. "Darling," she said, "Jacques is here to say good-bye. Surely you'll let me at least say good-bye to him? Surely I owe him that?"

"I don't know," I said. "I have nothing to do with it."

"Camilla," my mother started, and then she changed her mind about whatever it was that she had been going to say, and said instead, "Go in and say good-bye to him. Tell him I'm waiting in the hall for him. Then go in to Luisa."

It was a long time since I had heard mother speak

with such authority, and I obeyed her. I went into the living room. None of the lights were on and Jacques stood by the window looking out over the city.

"I've come to say good-bye," I said.

Oh, good-bye, good-bye, oh, Frank, good-bye.

He turned around and held out his hand. "Good-bye, Camilla, darling. This business has been hard on you, too, hasn't it?"

I did not answer.

He looked very sadly into my face and for the first time I didn't have it in me to hate him. "It's a very difficult thing to realize that your parents aren't the completely perfect human beings that parents ought to be, isn't it?" he said. "And I include your father in that statement as well as your mother. As for me, I'm not your parent, so there wasn't ever any reason for me to be perfect, was there? Well, good-bye, Camilla. Till we meet again, if we ever do." He dropped my hand then and went out to my mother in the hall. There was no place for me to go except to my bedroom, where Luisa was waiting.

Luisa was standing, as Jacques had been, by the window, only she had turned on all the lights; and if she was seeing anything out the window it must have been through and beyond the reflection of the room in the black glass. When I came in she handed me a letter. "Here," she said. "Frank told me to give this to you. I wasn't going to give it to you at all. I was going to throw it away. But then I— Here it is."

I took the letter without saying anything and turned my back to her and opened it.

"Camilla," it began starkly. "Bill and Mona are busting up. I'm going with Bill to Cincinnati. Luisa's staying with Mona. So that's that. I can't say good-bye to you. Do you know why? You'll just have to know. I can't write what I feel, either. You'll just have to know that too." He had signed it, "Love, Frank," and the "love" was written in a hurried, shaky way, as though it was a difficult word for him to write.

I folded the letter and put it back in the envelope.

"Frank told me to take the letter up to you at school," Luisa said. "He said to be sure I got it to you before school was out."

"Oh."

"I'm sorry," Luisa said. "I guess I wanted you to be unhappy too."

"That's all right," I said.

"I'll see you tomorrow at school."

"All right," I said.

"Do you think you could get there early? I mean if you're going away soon too—"

"All right," I said again.

"I have to go back to Mona now. She needs me. She didn't want me to leave at all but I said I had to bring you Frank's letter. Well—good-bye."

"Good-bye," I said.

I turned out all the lights and I went over to the window. Lights were on in most of the windows across the court, and above the buildings the sky was dark and clear and a single bright star was throbbing against the blackness. I did not wish on it because at this particular moment there wasn't anything left to wish. I held Frank's letter in my hand, and I knew that I would always have it to look at and to keep, and that now I did not have to try to forget him.

But I knew I could not read it again yet, and that for a while at any rate I would not be able to think of him.

I looked at the roof of the smaller building, but there was no one there, no lonely woman leaning over the parapet, no one to stand there to watch the moon rise over the broken edges of the city, no one to kiss there in the dark the way I had seen my mother and Jacques kiss.

I looked back at the star and it pulsed and throbbed with living light and all of a sudden my eyes filled with tears and my chest was choked with sobs.

No, I said to myself sternly. No, Camilla.

Betelgeuse, I told myself with anger, Betelgeuse is in the constellation of Orion, the Hunter. It is the first star whose diameter was measured. It is three hundred million miles in diameter and it is five hundred light-years distant.

I told myself these facts and the tears retreated and I knew that I would not have to cry.

ABOUT THE AUTHOR

Madeleine L'Engle is the author of numerous books, including the Newbery Award–winning *A Wrinkle in Time*, *A Wind in the Door*, and *A Swiftly Tilting Planet*. Her most recent novel, *A Ring of Endless Light*, the third volume of the Austin Family Trilogy, including *Meet the Austins* and *The Moon by Night*, was named a Newbery Honor Book. Madeleine L'Engle lives in New York City with her husband.